"Is Something Funny Mr. Allen?"

Dedication

To Liz Hobbs Rhandi
for her support and kindness
during the writing of this book.

To Kathy Kempton, my dearly loved wife
who turned "No you can't" into "Yes you can."

Even though I invented Richard Allen, he became as real to me as anyone I can name. His struggles with love, friendship, and the adults around him reflected my own. I did my best to be true to his thoughts and feelings. I know you'll fund a laugh or two and some tears as you read this coming of age story and find yourself, people you know, and some memories. Please enjoy.

Ron Kempton

Contents

Chapter 1

THE BUS RIDE HOME

Hi, my name is Richard Allen. Chronologically, I'm 13 years old. In my head? Well, my mom says I have the soul of an old man. I guess I look at everything from an overly-analytical point of view. I said that to my grandpa one time and he told me I was being smug. I looked up "smug" in his dictionary and when Mom found out, she made me write a two page essay on "Why you shouldn't look up stuff your grandpa says."

It's 1974 and President Nixon has his can in a sling. When I found out that the President had an advisor named Bebe Robozo, nothing surprised me. I don't look, it makes my stomach ache. I pay little attention to the mad world. I just don't understand people or being 13. I hate it, to tell you the truth. What's worse is going to school. OK, I confess I like to read. I read a lot and I'm good at science. Other people... what can I say? It's like this: If the other kids at school were even bigger idiots than they already are, I'd have to beg my folks to send me to some bizarre third world country where kids eat insects and their chores include helping the village priest shrink heads.

Take what happened to me the other day. Friday, to be exact. The bell rang for lunch. You should see this! The hallways are pulsating with thousands of the most antisocial, pre-pubescent, trouble-seeking "hellions," as my mom would say, on earth. Or possibly any other planet now that I think of it. I don't compete. I just wait near the top of the quad with Marty Shale. He's my only friend. I like having just one friend. It keeps life simple and Marty, well, he's a dyed-in-the wool quick-witted wise guy. As smooth and cool as it gets. He's long and lean with a head full of pitch-black hair. This guy "can't" keep his mouth shut. It isn't in him. Last week, our homeroom teacher, Ms. Dang, was taking attendance. When she called Marty's name, instead of saying "Here," he *belched* "Here!" Then I got in trouble for laughing.

"Is something funny Mr. Allen?" Ms. Dang said as loud as she could.

"Well, yes."

To teach me not to laugh at Marty, she sent me out of the classroom. I always thought it was odd to punish someone by making them leave a place they didn't want to be in the first place. So I stood outside until she decided that I was human enough to let back into class. I would find myself in that position because of Marty more than once. Marty thought it was a riot that I got sent out of the room for something he did. I still thought it was funny, so I don't know what I learned. It just went like that. Marty would act out. I either got into trouble or had to explain why he was nuts.

Marty spent an awful lot of time in the principal's office. The principal's name is Mr. Reichfeld. The kids call him "The Third Reich". He doesn't smile. As a matter of fact, his face was locked in a never-ending grimace. I didn't blame him. If I became the principal at this school, I'd stick my head in an oven and call it a day. Anyway, Marty and Mr. Reichfeld knew each other very well, and Marty seemed to take pride in it.

So what about last Friday? It started during lunch, like I said. Me and Marty were hanging in the quad, waiting for the initial rush of "hunger-crazed alien space seeds," as Marty called them, to ebb. The cheerleaders always practiced on the grass near the lunch area.

The coach, Mrs.Tendal, had a mega-phone she used to yell commands at them. Marty stood behind her and did the drills with them. Mrs. Tendal never said anything to him. I guess she figured as long as he's not doing any real harm, who cares?

Needless to say, most of the girls in school hated Marty's guts. Since we did everything together, they lumped us in the same category. If Marty was a loud, crude, jerk, - then so was I. It didn't bother me much, except in one case: Wendy James. Up until the day she walked into our math class, humans were a necessary evil, a source of constant irritation. Wendy was different. The first time I saw her every nerve in my body did somersaults. I got all steamy inside my shirt and Marty says I turned three shades of puke red. Watching her walk across the schoolyard was a daily religious ritual. I literally thanked God as she lithely swayed from one side of the quad to the other.

At those moments, my whole being was fixed on her as she passed, like an angel, with the spring breeze gently lifting her hair and tossing her skirt. When the moment passed, I would look at Marty and groan, drop my head onto his shoulder and beg him to take me out now. He would pat me on the back and say, "Mating season will pass, and it will soon be just a hazy memory from the days of yore." He always collected words I found in books I was reading. I didn't get how he remembered them, but it was too funny to question.

Anyway, it wasn't that simple. It wasn't lust. Oh no, lust is easy. This was something I'd never known. It went deep. "Marty will you kill me after lunch?" I moaned.

"What's wrong with right now, Romeo?" He teased me about her, but he knew not to go too far.

Lunch was an exercise in unbridled insanity. First of all, Marty never bought lunch. I would buy lunch and he would eat it! The yard dog was an old lady named Mrs. Ellie. Marty swore she was a hundred and ten years old and lived in a rest home with her eighty-five-year-old daughter. He had a theory that they were alien spies trying to take over the town by turning everyone's kids into Nazi aliens.

In his own off-center way, Marty made lunch seem a little, but only a little, more bearable. Anyway, kids were everywhere. Throwing food, girls screaming, and Walter Lemming running across tables doing belly flops in everyone's mashed potatoes.

The only time the circus subsided was when Coach Daniels came out of the locker room followed, as always, by about half the football team. I always protested the actions of any student who used influence with their teacher to muscle everyone else around. I mean, you never saw the Chess Club acting like they ran the school! In all my thirteen years I don't think I ever saw anyone in the Entomology Club strutting around campus with their teacher, making people move out of the way when they came down the hall! But there they'd be, with the coach. Even Marty knew not to push this guy around. Coach Daniels was a jock's jock, muscular to the degree of impossible. When he came into the lunch area, the din of noise went down to about a thousand decibels. If you messed with him? Well, Marty said he saw Coach Daniels rip a kid's arm off with his eyebrows one time. I knew that it was a pant-load, but it seemed like a good idea to believe it. So there we were. I hated jocks, and I hated P.E. I didn't want to stay in the lunch area with them. But Marty was finishing my lunch, and I was still in a depressed love-haze over Wendy James.

Then it happened. Miss Ellie came over and accused Marty of throwing his tater tots at Martha Horowicz. Marty really didn't seem to mind getting "in a mess," as he called it, over something he actually did. But he did NOT like, and would NOT accept being falsely accused! I tried to stand up for him, but she had her mind made up. Marty was red-faced with anger. He argued and fought until Coach Daniels heard the fracas and came over to put an end to it. The coach grabbed Marty's arm and said, "You again, Shale? One of these days they're going to haul you off for good!" Coach Daniels drug Marty out of the lunch area to the cheers of the football team. I had made up my mind to be a witness for Marty, but my attention was stolen by a couple of jocks who came over to our table to rub salt into the wound.

"What happened Twitchy Richie? Did your girlfriend finally get what's coming to him?" What could I do? I was smaller than them, out-numbered, and out-gunned. "I asked you a question, Freak."

His name was Mark DeVerge. He was the quarterback and team leader. He thought he was Ken Stabler.

"He didn't throw anything," I squeaked.

He put his finger in my face and warned me of the "weird flesh ripping mutilation" I was going to get "as soon as school ends today!" I turned and headed for the office. I looked over, and there stood Wendy James. At that very moment I discovered my ego. I turned bright red and slumped away. My legs felt like boiled asparagus. I had to cross the quad to a barrage of catcalls and crude comments from the jock-shlocks behind me. I never thought I'd say this, but I was glad to get to the office. As soon as I walked through the door, there sat Marty. His lips were pinched into a knot and his eyes were all watery. The principal's office is actually down a long hall. The room we were waiting in was full of secretaries typing and telling stories about dinners they ruined.

"Did you see The Third Reich yet?" I whispered as I sat down next to him.

"NO!" he growled through his teeth. "I hate that jerk!" I looked around to see if anyone heard him. All was quiet.

"Everyone hates Mr. Reichfeld!" I said, laughing into his ear.

He looked at me and said, "I'm talking about my dad, not Reichfeld." Marty looked at me. "He won't talk to me. He treats my sister like she's invisible. He stays gone a lot, even on weekends." Marty's eyes filled with tears. "Even when he is home he won't even look at me." Marty wiped at his face with his shirt. "My mom just looks the other way. I think she drinks to avoid him. It's nuts! I can't stand being at home. I don't know if I can stay there anymore! I mean, my dad is such an idiot! He thinks I'm twelve. He doesn't even know I'm fourteen."

"You're fourteen?" I whisper-hollered. I felt mortified for him.

"Yeah. I flunked fifth grade." He looked the other way and sobbed. He looked at me. The pain was clear on his face. "Please don't tell anyone, please!" he pleaded. I couldn't speak. I just sat there and stared at him.

I was frustrated for him and speechless. Then he looked at me and asked, "What's your dad like, Richard?"

I went blank. My brain was flooded with pieces of things I couldn't put together, parts of things I thought might apply, but I was just lost for an answer. "I really don't know." I sort of whispered, staring out past him.

"Hello, Marty," came a gruff voice from above us. I looked up and there was Mr. Reichfeld. He reached out, gave Marty's shoulder a manly squeeze, and patted him. "You having a hard day, Son?" I sat stunned. His voice was calm and friendly. I guess he knew way more about Marty's home life than I did, he seemed like he really cared. "Why don't we go into my office, Marty, and see if we can work this out?" He got up and walked away with "The Third Reich." I sat there utterly turned inside out.

All of us know that the powers rule. Just or unjust, I wasn't going to stand up for Marty and now my soul was being twisted by a tornado I could not understand. Why couldn't I answer a question about my own father?

Why didn't I know him? I was in such turmoil I even forgot about the flesh ripping mutilation I was supposed to receive from the football team, Wendy James was the last thing on my mind. I walked toward the parking lot between the junior high and the high school, lost in serious and damaging thought. I couldn't go to my last class. I felt kind of sick and lonely in a weird way, so I just wandered. I spotted Lance Cawlings, the coolest guy in both schools. He was out by his car. He's into the Allman Brothers and talks a lot about Edgar Winter. He was changing the strings on his Gibson Les Paul. He liked me because I would come and talk to him about music and ask him questions. He looked over at me as I walked up and said, "Hey Hip Rich, what's up, man?"

"Lance?" I blurted out without thinking. "Do you know your dad?" He stood up straight, leaving off his guitar, and looked at me.

"My ol' man was killed in a gambling hall in Memphis when I was in sixth grade." I stared at him in utter disbelief. He looked around to see if anyone was there. "OK, listen man, and don't repeat this to anyone."

"My dad was a trucker. He left Sacramento on his way back home. This happened when I was like, ten, 'ya know? So he stops at a truck stop near Fresno to use the facility. Well, when he was on the toilet, he had a heart attack and died. I'm a musician, Man, I can't tell people my dad died on a toilet!"

"So you chose a gambling hall in Memphis?"

"Well, it sounds cooler than dying on a toilet in Fresno!"

He shrugged his shoulders and went back to re-stringing his guitar. Lance seemed to forget I was there, so I meandered over to the front of the school where the buses picked up and let off the kids every day. There were some boulders there, so I got up and sat down on one to wait for Marty. It was bad enough that everything around me was insane. But then I came to realize I didn't even know my own father! Then I wondered if he knew me. That really threw me. I think he says stuff, but most of the time he's just talking to all of us. I have an older and a younger sister who are always crying and throwing themselves around. My mom calls them "drama queens." I don't know if dad talks to them or not.

About a month before, Dad said something to one of the girls and she ran into her room crying and shouting, "You don't care! No one cares!" Then my dad got a lecture from my mom about hormones. This, however, didn't come close to being asked what my dad is like, and not knowing the answer. It was just another unending question that I thought would plague me forever. I was deep in what seemed like futile analysis when the school bell rang.

OK, there's this really old movie my grandpa likes. It's called "How the West Was Won." My folks make me watch it with him about once a year. There's this scene where the Indians cause a buffalo stampede. That's pretty much what it was like at the end of the school day. Only, buffaloes are more civilized than the throng of Twelve to Seventeen-year-old maniacs that flooded the front of the school at 2:45 PM Monday through Friday, September to June.

It's a nightmare in motion. If the unbelievable quagmire of adolescent insanity wasn't bad enough to watch, there was an unparalleled horror that I refused to face at all costs! The dreaded Bus Ride Home. I would have rather walked three miles home than ride the bus.

There were tons of kids who lived near the school and walked. Every day on their way home, they would flood into a little mom and pop hamburger stand about a quarter mile from the school. It's called "Little Eddie's Big One, biggest burgers in the world." On top of the building, there was a giant neon sign of a little guy shoving a hamburger in his wide-open mouth. The burger was about ten times bigger than he was. I never could figure out how he made a burger that huge. How did he get that much hamburger into his mouth? Where did he get buns that huge? Did he have his family help him hoist burgers onto the grill? What about onions and tomatoes? Were they that big so they could fit inside? How much mayonnaise and mustard did he need to spread on the bread? Did Guinness know he eats hamburgers that big? It made me crazy.

The only time I went there, Marty and I got into a row with the guy behind the counter. I asked if he was happy working at a hamburger stand. He came at me and said, "How would you like a fist burger, Mini-Mouse?"

Marty shot back in his cool, flip way, "Is that on the menu, Zitzilla?" The guy leapt over the counter and Marty ran. I was left there to explain that Marty was a homeless recluse and my family was looking out for him while he went through rehab. Even that is better than taking the bus. It may sound like an ongoing narrative from a Labor Day "Twilight Zone" marathon, but walking up those three steps onto the bus was a trip into the darkest corners of limbo. The insanity of watching kids load onto their various buses is worth telling.

First of all, the bus drivers can't open the doors until 3 PM. By this time, every other kid in school, along with their buddies, is huddled in what looks like five blobs of undulating stupidity that no human should see. They jump, spit, scream, chase, slug, and annoy each other like a bunch of war-crazed Barbarians.

Then, the unthinkable happens. The bus opens its doors and a wall of adolescent flesh pushes forward in what seems like an attempt to squish about eighty kids through an opening that could only fit one. They cuss, bully, hit, pull, and squeeze their way through a portal too small for this activity in a daily dance of mindless absurdity that can't, and never will, accept supervision.

I got up and walked along the line of buses. At the rear of the last bus, I looked up and saw Todd Mitchells. He had three of his buddies block him from the view of the bus driver's mirror. He pulled his pants down and smashed his can up against the rear window. Dale Bitters saw me and smashed his tongue against the window. Kate Ridgeway walked by and said, "Hi Richie."

She's cool. She plays golf and she's different from the rest of the monkeys' butts crammed onto these rolling shriek-fests. Bus 24 got hung up 'cause the guys outside, in what was supposed to be a line, started a small riot. Paul Gimmer got a bloody nose and ended up duking it out with Larry Utters right inside the bus! It took about ten minutes before the yard dogs got a handle on it and hauled them away, God knows where.

Finally, the five busloads of mindless screaming idiots pulled away. This was when I began to wonder. What profane act of social criminality does someone have to commit to be sentenced to driving a school bus? I'd rather be thrown into the lowest pits of the Chateau d'If, than be a bus driver. Nothing made sense. Especially the gnawing feeling that I had no idea who my father really was. It's like he was there, but I just didn't know him. I had no answer for the question that Marty had asked me about my own dad. What is he like? How could I not know my own dad? Marty ran up and slugged me in the arm.

"What happened?" I asked, rubbing my arm.

"I have to shave my head and report to Miss Ellie for a frontal lobotomy. She wants me to begin training as one of the Nazi aliens preparing to transport humans to their planet. They take you there so you can make tweezers and wash dishes for the alien queen."

"Marty! I mean, for real?!"

My questioning did no good. He stiffened his arms and started walking around like an alumnus of the alien cursed. He began speaking in some voice that was supposed to sound like an alien.

"I have alien detention for two weeks on planet Death Rain!"

"What!? You didn't throw anything!" I objected.

"I argued with the yard dog! Reichfeld says I need to learn how to handle things without getting angry. Besides that, it's better than being at home,"

He left off his strange charade. We hung out and debated about me waiting for him to get out of detention for two weeks. The time got away from both of us.

"I suppose it's too late to walk home now," I grumbled.

"I get in trouble if I get home after four-thirty. Then again, I pretty much get in trouble for everything," he laughed.

We both turned and stared mournfully at the after-school activity bus. We sauntered toward the gates of doom, stepping slowly onto the bus with the rest of the after-school stragglers. As I walked up the steps of the bus, I glanced at the bus driver. He was an old guy with an eye patch sitting there in a catatonic state that made Mt. Rushmore look like a rock concert.

"I haven't been on a bus in two years!" I moaned to myself.

But I felt sorry for Marty and his bizarre afternoon of unjust treatment. I felt sad at the plight of the catatonic bus driver, but looking at him drove me mad. I sat across the aisle from Marty so I couldn't see him. I was turned sideways looking over Marty's shoulder. No sooner did I get myself turned around than Marty's face took on a look of amused but sympathetic surprise. Somehow I knew what his look meant, but I couldn't allow myself to dream that big. I sat there and watched Marty's eyes until they stared up to his right side. My heart knew. All that had been awakened inside told me the story. What I longed for and feared the most was right next to me. I turned my head and looked. It's weird the way life has a way of humiliating you into reality. I wish I could have a do-over, but life has a weird sense of humor and do-overs never happen. When I said, "Hi Wendy," my voice cracked. If I could have managed to live out the rest of my life inside an athlete's shoe, I would have. But there was simply no place to hide.

Then Marty said, "Hi Wendy!" and made his voice crack *on purpose*. I should have killed him right there, but somehow it eased the tension. The bus rolled away. Marty jumped up and sat in front. Wendy sat in the seat Marty vacated on the opposite side. It wasn't long before we got to Marty's stop. "See 'ya!" he hollered as he ran and jumped off the bus.

She sat there, so gentle and feminine that my heart just melted. She looked down as she adjusted her backpack in her lap. Without lifting her head, she looked up at me. Her brown eyes caught mine, and then she smiled. "Those jock-shlocks were pretty rough on you today." She called them "jock-shlocks!" I was so in love with this girl I would've eaten a handful of gravel if she asked me to.

"Yeah, well, I guess they changed their minds." I'm sure that I was speaking, but I could barely hear my own voice.

"Oh, really?" she laughed. "Well I guess someone told the coach how they treated you in the lunch area after he hauled Marty away. Now who do you think would tell on them like that?" She looked at me with an I-know-something-you-don't-know look on her face and smiled.

"Well, what happened?"

She told me the coach made them come to practice an hour early for a lecture and calisthenics. I was mesmerized. Not by the fact that she clearly got me out of a flesh ripping mutilation, but while she was talking, she took her lipstick out of her backpack and put it up to her lips.

Then she pinched her lips together and said, "I just don't know who would treat those dorky jockstraps like that."

She was as coy as she could be. When she looked at me, all I could do was sit there. I think my mouth was hanging open, but I'm not sure. She got a little nervous and asked, "Do you think you could walk me home from my bus stop, Rich?"

I suddenly realized I was having frontal lobe meltdown! She called me "Rich." Not "Richard" or "Richie" but "*Rich*." I do not know what kept me from exploding. My mind raced, my skin got all tingly, my feet started getting all sweaty, and my hands were shaking. I wanted so bad to play it cool, but I didn't know what to do.

So I worked up this dorky cool guy voice and said, "Why, sure." She smiled, and then something happened I'll never forget as long as I breathe. She leaned forward to take her shoes off and her blouse fell forward. My eyes darted in a thousand different directions. What could

I do? A thousand feelings rushed me from every which-way. I looked and then quickly looked away. She seemed not to care, or was unaware, or whatever.

I was trying to be good, but I couldn't. Some unseen force was controlling my eyes. Not that I was looking. I couldn't help but . . . She sat up, pulled her knees up, rested her elbows on her knees, leaning toward me, said, "You're shy, aren't you?"

"Sometimes, I guess."

"Well, I like shy boys. I want to be a dancer when I get out of school. It's my dream, being a dancer. What's your dream, Rich?" When she said my name, I got all warm inside.

"I haven't given it too much thought, I just try to get through each day with as much sanity left over as I can."

She smiled, "Yeah, junior high is so bogue."

Oh Man! This girl wasn't just gorgeous. She had a mountain of personality to go with it! After that, the conversation flowed. I hardly noticed the bus stopping and letting us off. We walked slowly, and I savored every minute of it. I dreamed about seeing her tomorrow, and thought about asking her to a dance or a movie or something. We got to her house way too soon for me. She sighed and said, "Thank you, Rich. I hope we can see each other again soon."

She walked up her driveway. I just stood there, watching her. I found my head swaying from side to side. As she got to her front door she turned, wiggled her fingers, and called out, "Bye Rich. See ya Monday!"

The way her eyelashes floated when she smiled, the way she pulled her hair back into a ponytail, the way she said my name, all of it made the two mile walk back to my house seem like nothing. I would have walked a thousand miles to be with her for one second.

When I got home, my dad was already there. I suddenly came back to earth and remembered my reason for skipping my last class. It seemed like a lifetime ago that Marty asked me what my dad was like. There he stood, poking through his desk in the den, looking for a #2 pencil.

"Honey, where's my real pencils? I hate mechanical ones," he said to himself. He looked up and saw me. "Oh hey, Richard!" he said, smiling. I didn't want my dad to be a stranger. "Is your mother out there?"

He was still in looking-for-pencil mode. I wanted him to see me so bad. I wanted him to talk to me. I just couldn't think of how to say anything. I started to speak. What? I don't know. Before I could open my mouth, my mom came into the room. She was still dressed up from doing business all day. When dad saw her he grinned and said, "Well, look at you, you fox."

He spoke in sort of a whispery, slick voice. I think he forgot I was there. He put his arms around Mom and started kissing her.

"Lee! The kids!" Mom whispered.

Then Dad looked at me and said, "He's a young man. It's no secret that his parents love each other."

Mom kissed Dad, said "Later" into his ear, handed him a pencil, and turned to leave the room. He watched her all the way. When she reached the door, she turned, wiggled her fingers at him, and winked.

"Man, I love it!" he called out, smiling.

It was then it came rushing in on me. Dad felt the same way about Mom that I did about Wendy James! WOW. He was young once, and single. Somewhere, at a party, a school dance, a club, a bank, I don't really know. At some point, my dad looked across the room and was floored by a beautiful girl. An angelic creature, just like Wendy! Now I could answer the question: "What's your dad like?" He's just like me, or I'm just like him.

I felt complete as I walked into my room. But this feeling wouldn't last very long. I guess dads are more of a mystery than I thought. I was shattered to pieces when I got to school on Monday and found out that Wendy's mother was transferred to Colorado by her employer. Wendy was gone, and it would be a long time before I saw her again. Marty tried, but I was not going to come out of this funk by his antics or any other means. This is when, and why, a chasm developed between me and my dad that lasted more than a few weeks. As a matter of fact, it went on for years, just when I thought I'd gotten to know him. Just when things seemed good.

I did not want to finish eighth grade or even go to school. Not only did I continue my overly-analytical questioning of everything, but now I was angry. I knew I liked Wendy a lot and I think she really liked me too. I went home that night thinking my dad would fix it. He knew what it meant to have the woman you love on your arm. Boy, was I wrong! That night I told him about Wendy and what happened. He looked at me and said, "Geez Bud, I guess that's the way the cookie crumbles."

He gave me a slap on the shoulder and went to his office like it was no big deal. I went to my room to try and figure out what "cookie" he was talking about!? Mom didn't usually make any cookies and the ones she did make didn't crumble. I started thinking maybe a glass of milk might go well with that stupid comment! What if Mom moved away and I said that to him?

"Well, Dad, I guess that's the way the cookie crumbles." Maybe he had a bad day. Maybe I talked to him at the wrong time. I decided to try again. I headed to his office and in so doing, had to walk past my older sister Samantha's room.

"Hey, Romeo, heard you lost your lover!" She yelled as I walked by.

How she knew anything about it came to me in an instant. My dad! The ensuing battle brought Mom and Dad into Sam's room to clear the field.

"My God, Richard, what has gotten into you?" Mom said, as she dragged me from the killing zone.

I yelled at my dad as Mom escorted me to my room. "You don't know me! You're a traitor!"

This brought Dad to my room. "Look, Richard, the whole world isn't going to stop 'cause one of your little friends moved away. Now get over it, Mister!" He stormed out.

Mom looked at me. "What is this, Richard?" she said softly as she stroked my hair. I sat on my bed and stared at the wall.

"Wendy's gone and my life sucks," I moaned.

Mom just left the room. I guess she figured I'd had a bad day and I'd get over it. I laid back on my bed and suddenly remembered, my eighth grade science project was due in a week. The next day at school

Marty revealed that he made a potato gun for his project. I was stunned, yet fascinated. I wanted to see it, but Marty refused to unveil his "secret weapon." "I'm calling it 'Deathspud'!" he said, with an evil slant in his eyes.

This started a series of events that would stun the whole school. I told him my project would be a visual explanation for why people over twenty are numbskulls. I was good at science. It involved analyzing and that was my forte. I was among the lovelorn, but no one cared. My dad said he would help me with my project but I did it myself.

Having him help me felt like a fight waiting to happen. Anyway, I already knew what to do. I slapped together a backboard out of some plywood and stapled some cloth to it to make it look like I gave a crap.

The only thing I could think of was Wendy. I got pretty heavy sighs at the dinner table when I mentioned her name. My other sister Lyn, who was only a year younger than me, said she pitied me for my loss and felt sorry that I was in such a state. I didn't know if she was being sarcastic or not. So I just went to my room and ate by myself.

The week went by quickly, and the Science Fair was set for Friday night. Mr. Erkle, the science teacher, wanted to draw the biggest crowd possible. Me and Marty got a ride from my sister Samantha. She wasn't too happy about wasting her Friday on the "Two Fosbots from Planet Dork." She made sure we knew it all the way to school. I told Mom and she said, "Well, the girls have it rough." That threw me for a loop that lasted 'till I was in the last year of high school.

Anyway, Marty had 'Deathspud' covered, and wasn't going to unleash his godless weapon until the last second. When we got inside, we were greeted by the Junior High Science Club. Jay Weber and Marty hated each other's guts.

Jay was the spokesman for the welcoming committee. We walked in and Jay said, "Greetings, science enthusiasts, and welcome to this year's Science Fair."

Marty shot back, "Hey Jay! What did you do for your science project? brush your teeth?"

Before Jay could come back, we were whisked into the room and shown the table where we would set up our projects. I started to put my board up and remove my science project from its carrying case, which was an old burlap sack I found in our garage. Marty proudly uncovered his weapon, loaded and ready for war! He took great pains to paint and put together a potato gun that looked like a space bazooka.

It was absolutely mind-blowing. The barrel was fire engine red, with a glossy black sight at the end. There were various gadgets fixed on the gun that didn't do anything, but looked great! The handle was made from a squirt gun and fixed up inside the back end of the barrel. It was red with black swirls. This thing was so cool it caught the attention of everyone. People were gasping. Kids were flocking over to touch it and ask if they could hold it. The ones that got to hold it had their parents take pictures.

Unfortunately, it also caught the attention of Mr. Erkle. He came hurrying over and hissed, "Mr. Shale! Are you not aware that weapons, especially potato guns, are prohibited from this event? Didn't you read the rules?"

"I think I lost that page." Was Marty's response.

I was moving back just to stay clear of what I could see coming. Mr. Erkle got real ticked off and grabbed the potato gun from Marty. When he did his finger hit the trigger.

BOOM!!!!!

I estimate the speed of the potato to be about six hundred miles a second. It hurtled past Mark DeVerge as he was ducking, blasted through Elaine Morese's project, which was an experiment to show the strength of glass under pressure. Her windowpane shattered like a piece of fine china in an expensive restaurant. The potato continued its flight across the gym and tore the living crud out of Jeremy Pruitt's real-life volcano. The slimy red goo that covered the judge's table was smelly and filled with chunks of mashed up potato. Marty ran out the door, who knows where? The problem was, he left me standing there! Mr. Erkle was beyond furious. He was ready to kill someone, and he looked right at me.

There are few things, when you're a kid, that are more insane than watching the adults around you implode. Mr. Reichfeld came over, took the potato gun away from Mr. Erkle and said, "Come on." The two of them disappeared. I looked over at Mark DeVerge and something happened that changed my life forever.

Even though it took a while. When I Looked at him, he smiled a knowing smile at me, and gave me the big thumbs up. It turns out that Mr. Erkle had been acting strangely ever since his wife abandoned ship. He got into trouble once for threatening another teacher. About a week before the science fair, he told Reichfeld to "Watch out! You never know what might happen next." I think he may have been talking about life in general, but along with the other weird stuff he did, it sounded way off base to our principal.

As it turned out, Mr. Erkle got blamed for the whole thing! It was his responsibility to approve all science projects ahead of time. He didn't. Marty's name never even came up! Even so, Marty kept a real low profile for about a week. He swore there was an FBI van parked outside his house, that a couple of plainclothes officers were following him, and had his whole street under surveillance. But then our attention was turned to the last couple months of school and life got a little, but only a little, better.

Marty decided for summer he would build a raft and sail to Tanzania. I went to my room to look up "Tanzania."

"Hey Marto, you dumb butt, it's in East Africa. You can't get there in a raft."

Marty started yelling from the living room about making our own Twinkies and selling them to raise money for his journey. I took a quick look at some mail my mom put on my dresser and there was a letter addressed from Wendy James. I tore it open as fast as I could.

"Hey Rich, Sorry about the sudden move. My mom's company said that she could either go to Colorado or lose her job. We just got settled and I wrote to explain. Rich I really do like you. I wanted so badly for us to get to know each other. If I can I'll write or visit. I'm so sad I wish things were the way they should be. Love Wendy."

I was blown away with excitement. I forgot Marty was even there. I grabbed a notebook that was lying around and wrote her back right away:

"Dear Wendy, I'm so happy to hear from you. I hope you're alright. I was a little surprised at how suddenly you were gone. We can still see each other. I will save money and come to Colorado, just to see you."

I was thinking about how to end my note when Marty came in, looked at the notebook, and yelled, "Whoooooooohooo Hot-Shot! She found you!"

"I can still tell everyone how you almost got away with murder with Death Spud' Marty-boy." I tried to appear evil as I spoke.

Marty feigned a Russian accent, "What do you mean 'Almost' Comrade?"

He jumped up and ran out of the house. I couldn't do anything but float on a cloud. Once again, the adult world invaded my beautiful dream world. Once again, the insanity was beyond analysis. My mom and dad decided to have spaghetti for dinner on this particular Friday eve. The pasta was boiling, the sauce was simmering and the garlic toast was browning. Me and Lyn were all in and around the kitchen jousting with the forks. Samantha was complaining about the lack of social awareness we were displaying. My dad walked in, took a big whiff and said, "Oh boy! Italiano tonight." He walked over to the stove and looked at the boiling water. "Oh no!" he said, as Mom walked in.

"Is there a problem?" "Yes! You put oil in the spaghetti water. That's not the way to cook spaghetti!"

"I've told you a thousand times not to put oil in the water!"

"Well excuse me, Mama Celeste, but it keeps the noodles from sticking together." "They just get all oily," he snitted back.

The fix was in and the fight started. The next thing I know Mom and Dad are yelling at each other over stuff I didn't even know about. "You never get the right oil when you change the oil in the car!" Dad yelled.

"Look, if you don't like the way I do things do them yourself!" she shouted back and on it went.

The three of us jumped into the car and Sam drove us to Taco Bell. We got back about an hour later. Mom and Dad were in the dining room having a romantic dinner by candlelight. I looked at Samantha and Lyn and they looked at me. I swear when we left, I thought we might come home and find the homicide squad at our house looking over the crime scene. Instead, the folks are acting like a couple of giddy newlyweds. I went to my room and shut the door. I think most of the time, just going off by yourself is the best thing you can do. While I was lying there, thinking about how beautiful Wendy is, and trying to conceptualize a way to go to Colorado, the phone rang. It was Marty.

"Hey! Did you get the letter from school about our graduation gowns?"

"I don't know," I said. "I try to avoid anything pertaining to school while I'm pondering the universal veracity of conjoined souls intertwined in the dance of love." Marty hated it when I used multisyllabic phrases.

"OK, well, the school board decided to have us wear ankle length gowns this year, 'cause it's the one hundredth anniversary of something."

"So what, Marty? Don't you know it's just another excuse to get us back on that campus?"

"You know what I'm going to do?" he said.

"No, what?" At first I was uninterested, but as his plan unfolded I could only see the wonder and excitement of it.

"I'm not going to wear anything underneath my robe. I'm going 'commando.'" He wasn't joking. Or so I thought.

"Are you serious?" I asked.

He started laughing his guts out and hung up the phone. The idea of it struck me at once as funny, rather bizarre, and slightly Bohemian with a hint of rebellious disdain combined. Should I? Would I? I let the thought slither through the analytical pathways of my brain. Then I just went with the beauty of it, the simplicity of it, and the ease with which it made itself my only thought. I'm goin' with it, man! Au naturelle. Thus began my way down the path to another Friday drenched with the dregs of a bubbling cauldron only Poe could imagine.

The next three weeks went by rather quickly. Marty got in trouble for asking too many questions in our history class. We were reviewing the French Revolution when our teacher, Mrs. Crane, told us the guillotine was named after Joseph-Ignace Guillotine, a doctor who recommended it for executions. Marty went nuts. He raised his hand over and over asking questions about this guy's family.

"Mrs. Crane, do you know what his parents were named? I think it was Ed and Mabel. Ed and Mabel Guillotine." Mrs. Carne tried to encourage Marty to look into Guillotine's family origins. Then Marty started speculating about this man's brothers and sisters.

Marty told the class that Joseph had a brother and sister, twins named Eugene and Leovene and that they invented the rack. Then he took off on the practice of beheading. "How far did the heads roll? Could they still talk after they were beheaded?"

Mrs. Crane finally had enough when Marty asked if the French people recycled the heads. He was sent to see The Third Reich and I didn't see him again until graduation.

I guess I can be as stupid as the next guy. If I had seen Marty before the Friday graduation ceremony, I might have ascertained that he had no intention of going nude under his graduation gown! I was so caught up in the end of the school year and planning my strategy for not wearing anything under my gown that I didn't talk to or even see Marty until we were already at graduation. I just figured all systems were "go." During the graduation, I kept looking at him and nodding my head and laughing. Of course, with the last name "Allen," I was in one of the first rows to go up on stage and get my diploma.

The details go like this: Mr. Reichfeld didn't want the faculty to have to sit in the blazing heat of a long ceremony. So he had fans installed around and under the stage. We had the graduation on the football field. So, they had to rent a stage. Well, the stairs weren't connected to the stage. They were just pushed up close to it and the stage was in sections. As we walked up, Lisa Adders started waving her hands and dancing around on the stage. This caused the stage to move enough to make the fans blow from under the stage right up the back of my gown, which then blew straight up over my head! Everyone in the eighth grade class got a full-on look at my white, freckly posterior.

My sister Samantha filmed the whole gruesome event. That weekend, she invited all her friends over for what she called "Richard's Ugly-Butt Pizza Party." She showed the footage of my gown blowing up over my head about a thousand times. I pleaded with my dad to make her stop but he said that was my punishment for being such a dumb butt. The whole gang got a big laugh out of that.

I spent most of that weekend in my room. Marty called me his hero and sent me a picture he took from the middle of the crowd. Thank God, I turned just in time to keep from exposing my frontal ornaments, but there was no two ways about it. The whole school and every parent in town saw my butt. I can be thankful, for once, that Wendy was nowhere near me and my bare rear end! My other saving grace was summer. I really hoped no one would remember this by the end of summer, at least not anyone going to high school. I was determined to stay in my room and write to Wendy. As usual, it was not going to go as planned.

Chapter 2

THERE'S MORE TO LIFE THAN FOOD

It doesn't take long to figure out why there's only three years of junior high. It's because no intelligent, thinking creature could handle being anywhere near a junior high school for any longer than that. As a matter of fact, I think there's a law: Three years is the maximum sentence for anyone to be in or near a junior high school no matter what heinous crime they've inflicted on humanity. Marty says that they were going to make Hitler be a janitor at our school for the rest of his life and that's why he killed himself.

My dad finally took the film of my exposed bottom away from Samantha, who was discussing putting a picture of it on a billboard sign near our house. As I had hoped, summer got me and my overexposed vertical smile off the hot seat. The naked rear-end followed me for a long time. Girls would laugh when I walked by and guys started calling me "Smiley." But high school was a big deal for all of us. Most of the kids were more occupied with starting their freshman year than my naked can.

Anyway, I finished junior high and was ready for a summer of languishing in my room. Wendy wrote me letters every couple of weeks. She really helped me through the end of the school year, and when I say "helped," I mean once she even did my algebra homework for me and mailed it back when she was done. During the last semester, she sent me a picture of herself in her eighth grade graduation gown. I thought I was alone when I saw the photo of her. I stared in reverent astonishment, looked close and whispered, "Holy crap!" My sister Lyn was behind me on the couch. She went into convulsions and told mom I was taking the Lord's name in vain. I shouted back, "If the Lord saw this picture of Wendy, he'd say the same thing!"

That night I had to read Psalm 23 to my whole family after dinner. We weren't really religious, but my sister was going through a "spiritual" phase and my mom didn't want to discourage her. Dad came over later and had me show him the picture of Wendy. "Holy crap!" he whispered, but Mom and Lyn both heard him. I think Dad's punishment was different than mine. He didn't have to read anything, but he did have to apologize to Lyn, and Mom told him that they would discuss this more later.

Summer was on. My next educational experience was high school, but that was about two months away. This summer was going to be long. It started with an ugly scene when Marty's dad came home drunk and beat him up real bad. Marty ran away. No one saw him or heard from him for almost three weeks. Finally, Marty's Aunt Myrtle, his mom's sister, called and said Marty was with her. That's when pandemonium hit the windmill. Aunt Myrtle told Marty's mom that as long as that "puke drunk" was in the house, she was not going to let Marty go home. She said, "He's going to cause real hurt someday, someone beyond his own family." She had already got the Social Services involved and Marty's dad, Sam, was in a lot of trouble. Marty's mom, Gerti, agreed. She told Sam to hit the road! Sam called his brother, who everyone called Truck, and Truck told him he could live with his wife and him during the split.

Marty's Uncle Truck was missing a leg. The right one below the knee, as I recall. He said he lost it in "The war," but he couldn't ever remember which one. Sometimes he'd say, "'Nam, man." Then other times, "Korea, Brothah." Marty told me he really lost his leg in a car crash. He didn't want anyone to know 'cause he still thought people he met would dig a war hero and didn't want to look bad. Anyway, the whole thing sounded like a story from the Brothers Grimm to me.

I asked my dad if Marty could live with us and he said, "Good Lord, no! I've got two girls here!" I never could figure out if he meant that Marty might try something crazy with one of my sisters, or if Dad was up to his clavicle in chicks and couldn't handle another mess.

Marty was gone for the first four weeks of summer. As for me, my unending analysis of everything around me was worse than ever. People just drove me nuts. The Fourth of July was particularly insane 'cause my dad's family flew out for the weekend from New Rochelle. You know, that place where Rob and Laura Petry from "The Dick van Dyke Show" lived with their son, Richie, the token child? I thought they made that place up for TV, man! It took me a whole week to get up the sanity to just accept it and move on.

So my dad's brother is the progeny of my grandma's first marriage to a man named Levi Goink. After my uncle was born, Levi ran off with a woman who worked at the sewage department. They went underground and he was never heard from again. Then my grandma married Grandpa Steven Allen. My dad was born a year later. How this constitutes "family" I'll never know. My uncle's name is Lou Goink and he acts like it. What's weirder is my uncle brags about their close family ties all the time. He calls my dad little "Bro-Meister."

Anyway, this traveling cavalcade of LOUD people from back East and their two kids came blowing into our lives like the aroma from a tar truck re-roofing the neighbor's house on a hot summer day. This included a cousin named Sped and his sister who was two years older than me. Her name was Lucretia. I begged my dad to let me stay home from the Fourth of July picnic, but my sister Samantha spoke up and said if she and Lyn had to go, why should "Mr. Recluso Nerdy-Boy" get to stay home? Besides, she went on, "Lucretia likes Richard." I was always at the bargaining end of the two girls and my dad, and perpetually came up at the short end of the stick.

The day of the picnic started with my mom and Aunt Gail getting into a fight over the potato salad. My mom made some and Aunt Gail bought some at the store. Enough said? It went downhill from there. I sat and watched a group of people who are supposedly related turn into a camp of dueling harpies that could not find common ground. Uncle Lou kept saying, "Come on! It's all in the soup." I never have understood what that meant.

Sped sat there and whined all day about his feet and his allergy to grass. He counted his mosquito bites five hundred times and finally went and sat in the car. At which his father shouted every five minutes: "Come on Speedo!" Lucretia kept coming over to me and rolling her eyes.

She finally said, "I didn't really want to be here but it's better than the suburban non-reality I have to live in." I was so impressed with "suburban non-reality" that I went ahead and engaged. Boy, was I sorry!

"I didn't feel like doing this either." I told her. She must have felt like she found a fellow soul. Suddenly she was off to the races.

"You know, non-reality is the only reality that matters. I'm totally into metaphysics. I mean, think about it, Cousin. What if we're all part of a giant's dream and he wakes up? What is time? You can stand there all day and look at your watch, but you're not really even here in the first place, so what is it your watch is saying? It doesn't explain God as a person, or the cosmos as an entity. If we don't exist, then what is the difference? On 'Star Trek' Mr. Spock said that we use our senses to judge the reality of a given situation, and once we become convinced of that reality we abide by its rules. But if reality is a non-issue then there is no reality. We aren't even here Richard! We aren't even real."

Suddenly her mom spoke up and said, "Lucretia, your bra strap is showing, Honey." Lucretia went into a mad rage and spent five minutes howling at her mom that she is always embarrassing her to the point of death.

When she stopped, I heard Marty's voice say, "If you're not really here, how can you be embarrassed?" I looked around and there was Marty.

"What are you doing and how did you get here?" I asked him. Lucretia went storming off and sat in the car with her brother.

Marty said, "Every Fourth of July I go on a walk-about." He saw it in a movie that was set in Australia, and thought it sounded pretty cool. We stood there and watched the whole party turn into a nut-fest. There was another outburst about potato salad. It made Aunt Gail run over and sit in the car with her two kids.

Uncle Lou just went on like his whole family wasn't sitting in the car and insisted on cooking the steaks himself. He liked it "The manly way." Upon being served, I realized that meant still chewing its cud. The meat was so red and runny I got sick just looking at it. You can see why we didn't stay for the fireworks. I left with Marty and we walked back to my house. Here's the real killer. After they went back home, my dad came into the living room and said, "Well now, that was a wonderful visit." I almost flipped.

"Was Dad with us during this circus where the freaks ruled?" I thought. But I held back from raving 'cause my sisters were always on his side. It felt like me against them. All they had to do was tell Dad and I was shut down.

Marty finally went back home. His dad got a slap on the wrist, and Marty's mom forgave him. No one could believe the injustice but me. Adults have a different way they punish each other than the way they punish kids. But it worked itself out alright 'cause Marty's Aunt Myrtle refused to let Marty stay there. What's more, Marty didn't want to be at home. Not with his father there. On the last weekend in July, Marty moved in with his Aunt Myrtle. He seemed to be happier and we could finally start hanging out, and hang out we did.

One day, as we flopped around my house, Marty got it into his head that we should build a tree fort in a vacant lot around the corner from the mall. "There's only one problem with that concept," I told him.

"What is that, Poor Richard?" (He started calling me that because of a copy of "Poor Richard's Almanac" he found in my dad's library.)

"There are no trees in the vacant lot you're talking about, Marto."

"Easy fix. We can make one!"

"Only God can make a tree!" Lyn shouted from her room.

This lit a fire under Marty that wouldn't go out. We walked over to the vacant lot and Marty instantly dubbed it "Shale Land." We began collecting every scrap of plywood, chicken wire, and anything else we could find. Marty told Myrtle what we were up to, and she bought him four posts and some cement. He simply wouldn't stop. We worked our guts out for three weeks. I dug the post-holes with my dad's post-hole digger and Marty found some plastic sheeting to cover the roof. The more we worked and talked about what we were doing, the more stuff people gave us!

Mr. Clamset, who lived down the street from Myrtle, told us if we would clean out his side yard we could have anything we found. It was a goldmine of junk: Aluminum siding, thrashed but usable, a load of two-by-fours, and a roll of tar paper. I thought Marty was going to lose his mind. "Blood, sweat, and tears, Baby," Marty yelled at me all day. We worked hard, and built this odd structure near the far corner of the lot, which kind of sloped down. You could see it from the road, but no one paid too much attention.

We nailed, tied, roped down, lifted and pushed day after day. The Swiss Family Robinson would have been wild with envy. We finally finished. It took three-and-a-half weeks. It was beautiful, rope ladder and all. A tire for a widow frame, a roof covered with heavy tar paper, a pulley to lift water and other goods up to what Marty called "The Delivery Window." Both my sisters and Myrtle came to gaze in wonder at Shale Land. Here's the real killer. Once we finished, neither one of us ever went there again! But a lot of other people did. Me and Marty would find newspaper reports and hear things on a regular basis about kids getting busted for drinking there or making too much noise on a Saturday night.

One girl from across town got suspended for using the tree house for cheating in school. Apparently she set up shop in the tree fort and was charging kids to do their homework. Bobby Miller got a merit badge from his Boy Scout troop for spending a week there. The guy who owns

Hot Dog Heaven got caught using it for office space to avoid paying rent! Marty laughed until he almost died. It was a fun way to kill the summer. But school was coming on. August was half gone.

The end of July is a nightmare for me, 'cause the first week of August is my birthday. I can't stand my birthday. I started begging my dad when I was around nine to cancel it. He refused. He said it was more for my mom than for me. So there I was, in my room. I figured I'd stay there all day and escape being the center of attention. It didn't work, but this one was almost as weird as my tenth birthday. Let me relate.

When I was seven, my dad and I had a father and son day at the circus. I was flummoxed by the clowns. I hate clowns. They scare me out of my wits. On the way home, I asked him, "How do you get to be a clown?"

He said, "I guess they have clown schools, Son. I don't know." He was just blowing off a little kid question, but it drove me nuts. I spent four months driving my parents crazy with clown school questions. Is there a clown college? How do you get into it? Is there an entrance exam? Can you get financial aid? What about government grants? Are there old experienced clowns that teach young aspiring clowns the tricks of the trade? Can you get a master's degree in clowning? The final straw came when I asked my dad what a clown graduation was like. He got all ticked off and sent me to my room.

Anyway, I think my parents thought I was into the whole clown thing, so my mom hired a clown as a surprise for my tenth birthday. What a riff. This guy shows up, calls himself "Pee Wee the Clown." He was so drunk he could hardly walk. It took an hour for this stoned wag to blow up a balloon. You should have seen him trying to make it into a poodle. For his finale, he passed out and crushed the cake my mom made for me. It was in the shape of a question mark. Maybe now you can understand my aversion to birthday parties. But I did agree to let my mom and sisters give me a small gift and say something, and my folks left me alone as far as parties went. This time they brought me into my dad's office and sat me down.

I have to explain my dad a little. He likes his answering machine. He screens calls and says he can tell whether he wants to talk to someone by the sound of their voice. OK. So there we are, in his office, and Mom says, "Honey! Lyn bought you a gift and she's really excited about it."

I looked at my dad and said, "What is it?"

"Well, Richard, we will let her give it to you," my Dad said with a wink.

Lyn walked in holding a box, her face all lit up. "Richie, I got you this." She handed me the box. I felt myself getting red-faced and looked down. Right then, my dad's phone started ringing.

"Let the machine get it," he said, waving for me to go ahead and open the box. I lifted the lid and looked inside. It was a Bible.

"Oh wow …umm." I didn't know how to react.

While I was looking at it, Lyn said, "Read the inscription!" It said, "Richard, I love you. Hope to see you in Paradise." She knew I loved to read, so she figured she might save my soul by giving me a Bible.

Just then, Marty's voice blasted through the speaker on Dad's answering machine. "Pick up the phone, Zit-Face!!!"

My mom grabbed the phone and said, "Marty, I'll have Richard call you later." Then she hung up the phone. All eyes were on me.

"Thank you, Lyn, this is really great."

My dad said, "Your mom and I got you something."

Mom said, "It's not a gift you can put in your hand, Richard. It's something I learned at the real estate office. Honey, Wendy's mom is moving back into the house they left. Wendy's Aunt Rachel has been there since they moved away and now they're all going to live together. Her mom kept the house and rented it to her sister. Wendy's mom's name is Katie. When her sister Rachel lost her home. Wendy's mom let Aunt Rachel move in. Wendy flew out early to help her move in."

"Wendy is here?!" I said, almost whispering.

"Not exactly," Mom said. "Well, she's in town. I stood up, almost losing the Bible Lyn gave me. I fumbled it around then put it on my dad's desk. Did you ever feel like you were in your underwear and the whole world was looking in your window? Well, there I was, thinking about the most beautiful creature on this earth and anyone watching me could easily tell how I felt. My face got all flushed and I felt out of place.

"Wow, Romeo, I guess your mom didn't hang up the phone all the way, I heard the whole thing." It was Marty, listening in after my mom tried to hang the phone up.

Mom jumped at the phone and said, "Marty do you want to tangle with me?" With that, I heard the phone click and go silent.

Dad handed me an envelope and said, "She wrote you this, Richard." I opened it and looked at this whole room of people staring at me.

"Can I be alone?" I said.

"Holy cow, Richard! Every one of us already knows you're spazzed out about her, just read it." Sam was always on me. "Nice and loud, Brother, so we can all share in your joy," she quipped. Mom made everyone leave and I read Wendy's letter to myself.

"Hi Rich, I can't wait to see you! I will be back and forth for the summer, my mom needs me to help her as well. So hang in there, and I'll let you know. P.S. I know this is asking a lot but can you help my Aunt Rachel at the mall? I have to go back to Colorado tonight so I can help my mom pack and drive back here. I feel kind of like I'm imposing, but it would really help. Love, Wendy.

It wasn't too much to ask at all. Making a few extra points seemed like a good idea. I was wrong again

The walk to the mall was kind of long. I walked along, wondering how high school would be. I guess girls have different things to worry about than boys do. I thought that maybe they worried about what to wear and what kind of new girls would be there. I was stressing on the possibility of some weird initiation like a bunch of seniors making me run around the track with soda crackers under my arms and then making me eat them. Or being pantsed and having my jeans run up the flagpole.

Thinking over the new school year made the walk go a little faster. I got to the mall. There were cars everywhere. Inside was bizarre, to say the least. There was a half-off sale on all back-to-school items. They had a Kiddy Fair with small rides and games. Greta Delany's Dance School for Toddlers was having a recital. I knew this was a recipe for disaster the minute I walked in. You know how, when they have a prison riot on the news, what it looks like? That's nothing, man! A kid from school walked by, looked at me, and said, "I'd turn back if I were you!"

The main door takes you into the second level. There's a railing that surrounds an opening looking down at the lower level. Greta's Dance School had a stage set up on the inner edge by the Food Court. There were no seats. Moms, dads, aunts, uncles and grandparents with camcorders were all just kind of huddled around the stage. A small train tooled through the mall and stopped on the backside of the stage. Kids could get a ride around the mall for a dollar. The Food Court was behind the stage. That's where I was going to meet Wendy's aunt. The train left every fifteen minutes blowing a really loud whistle. I found out it wasn't loud enough.

I finally made it down by some unknown miracle. Wendy's Aunt Rachel started yelling at me across the Food Court, which embarrassed me out of my wits. I couldn't figure out how she knew me but I guess Wendy gave her a description. When I got to her, I was promptly introduced to Scooter, Wendy's cousin, He was wearing a mock military outfit and he was waving a G.I. Joe at me saying it has a kung-fu grip. All of ten years old, this kid would not stop eating. Shortly after the introductions, he was handed three corn dogs, a large order of chili cheese fries, and a large strawberry Fruit-o-Crazy Lemonade! He wolfed that down in about 8.6 seconds and kept yelling, "I want to be in the show!"

Wendy's aunt was always talking. I had a hard time keeping up because she talked so fast and I couldn't get around her hair. It was all bunched up in this Farrah Fawsett thing that was way too big for her head. She went on about a sewing project that got lost in the move. She kept asking me if I would watch Scooter while she did some last minute shopping. I kept making excuses hoping she would let it go, but she wouldn't. I finally agreed just to keep peace, a move I would regret for a very long time. . Scooter was demanding a cinnamon roll. His mom gave him twenty dollars and he ran to the other end of the Food Court. He was gone for about fifteen minutes and returned with a triple fudge chocolate swirl shake with vanilla chips, a ton of sprinkles and whipped cream on top.

I stood in amazement, feeling sick just looking at this shake. Then he pulled a cinnamon roll *out of his pocket* and started consuming it as well, lint and all. I looked up to see if Wendy's aunt had noticed, but she was long gone. Scooter inhaled the cinnamon roll and started whining, "I want to be in the show!" With that, he turned and darted toward the stage. I yelled after him, but he didn't stop.

"HEY! Come back here!" I called. I chased after him, but he reached the stage before I could. He jumped onto the stage with the ballerinas and started gyrating and jumping all over the place.

Greta started hollering, "Get down from there!" A security guard saw the nightmare unfolding and came across the walk, not noticing the train coming at him. The conductor blew his whistle but the guard didn't hear it 'cause of all the noise. The train had to swerve to miss him. It hit the back corner of the stage and the leg collapsed. The same side in front buckled under the strain. The ballerinas and Scooter all fell, rolling off the stage. Scooter's shake went flying out of his hand and landed on a huge power strip that was connected to the main power source for the whole mall. The lights in the mall all went off. Sparks started flying and caught the stage curtains on fire. I watched, completely stunned.

Right then, the theater let out. The people exiting the theater were just treated to "The Towering Inferno." Someone yelled, "FIRE!" and the slime hit the fan. I couldn't do anything but react. I grabbed the curtains, yanked them down, and they fell to the floor, putting out the fire. I got a tight hold on Scooter's arm and walked quickly as I could, trying not to be noticed, into the theater and out the back exit. The emergency trucks were just pulling in as we crossed the parking lot.

It just so happened, Wendy's Aunt Rachel was not too far outside the back of the theater, shoving bag loads of stuff into the back of her car. I was red-faced. Scooter ran to his mother. As she knelt down she said, "Oh poor Scootie! This has been so hard on you!"

I would live to regret this few minutes of my life, but sometimes things just happen.

Scooter looked at his mom and said, "I'm hungry."

I blew up and yelled, "Look, man, there's more to life than food! I can't believe Wendy asked me to do this!" "You didn't just say that," I thought to myself. Wendy's aunt gave me a look that should have killed me.

She looked at Scooter and said, "I think I have everything." Then, with one wicked glance in my direction, she shoved Scooter into her Gremlin and sped away. I felt a sure sense of doom for my outburst, but I could never have imagined what terrible events would visit my life in the days ahead.

I would soon find out that Wendy wasn't coming back as soon as I thought. I don't think even her mother could see what was next. Not only that, but Wendy's letters stopped coming after a few weeks. I would never have found out why if not for Mark and Marty.

Back at the house, things were quiet. Lyn went to a friend's house to spend the night. My sister Samantha was gone for the weekend with her friend, Tanya. I was glad they were gone for a while. At first, things went great. My dad was in his office and Mom was taking a bath.

"Richard, Son, it's almost eight and I have to be up early. Please keep the noise down" My dad's voice took over my fears of the events at the mall, and I was facing a grim reality. My mom always says, "Live and learn." Well, I was in the process of learning something I never thought about before.

Chapter 3

WIN, LOSE, OR DRAW

I asked my mom why I felt so weird.

"Richard I think you're in love," she cooed.

I turned red and went to my room. I was sure the week wouldn't get by without another letter from Wendy. Her trip back to Colorado should be over soon. Or at least that's what I thought. I begged my mom to call over and see when Wendy and her mom and brother would be arriving, but she kept forgetting. Finally I called myself. Wendy's aunt answered.

"Hello, this is Rachel."

I knew this wasn't going to be good. "Hi, this is Richard Allen. Can I leave a message for Wendy?"

There was a pause, a long one. "Now, who is this again?" she said.

"It's Richard Allen. I watched Scooter for you at the mall."

"Oh yes. Scootie told me how you lit the mall on fire and almost yanked his arm out of its socket. He said you threw his shake away and wouldn't let him finish it." She wasn't friendly to my cause and she wasn't going to be.

"Well it got pretty wild in there so......"

At that, she interrupted me and said, "I'm quite busy. What do you want?"

Suddenly, my nerves went nuts and I couldn't talk straight. I couldn't believe what I was being accused of. It just didn't happen that way. "I thought I might come and help you organize the house for Wendy, her mom, and brother for when they get here." I tried to sound cheery and helpful, but this was not going to fly.

"Well, my sister had to go to Texas and there's a fine young man named Carl Simms that lives on this street. Wendy and he are a fine match, and I'm sure we don't need any more help!"

With that, she hung up the phone. All I heard was "Texas" and "Carl Simms." My stomach turned to jelly and I glazed over. As long as Wendy's aunt was in control, I'd never see Wendy again. Carl Simms was one of those lanky guys, all arms and legs. Girls were always flocking around him like he was a movie star or something. Wendy's mom didn't really know me, so I couldn't call her at all. I had to rely on Wendy. I knew she would come through. But how could she when her aunt was controlling everything?

The week passed without any note, a phone call, or a sound from Wendy. It was time to get ready to go back to school. I was at the mercy of life for the first time. I was hopeful, but still my heart knew something wasn't right.

Marty was ready for school. It provided him with the perfect outlet for his humor. We did our schedules together so we could try to get as many of the same classes as possible. We planned to go and register together the following Monday.

I had a great time with Marty. We did the whole school plan at his Aunt Myrtle's house. She is one of a kind, crazy as a bat! Marty loves her with all his heart. He calls her "Myrt the Squirt." She's only four foot nine, but Marty says if you get on her wrong side, she's capable of pulling your face off your skull with a butter knife.

I left Marty's in a fine mood but things were about to change. I got back home. It was late afternoon, so I sat on the couch with a Ding

Dong and started checking the mail. There was a letter from Wendy. I shoved the Ding Dong into my mouth and started reading.

Dear Richard, We had to go to Texas. This is so rough on my poor mom. Her job isn't going well and they sent her to their Texas complex or something. A lot has changed in the last few days. My aunt said a lot of things about you to my mom. I wish I could talk to you. I don't know how long we will be in Texas. I have to sneak to write to you, I was barely able to get this note to you because of the things my aunt told my mom. Bye for now, Wendy."

My mouth hung open with Ding Dong dripping out of it. I sat there stunned out of my mind. I'm getting knifed in the back and I can't defend myself. I wanted to write to her but I didn't know where to write. My mom said to wait until things cooled down. I couldn't phone her, I didn't know where to call. I was stuck and school was about a week away. I felt dead.

My Wendy! I should have never said anything to her wretched, brat cousin, "The Eating Machine." I tried for hours to find a mailing address for her mom's company. I called the place where Wendy's mom worked when they lived here, but they wouldn't give out personal information. I was the victim of cruel lies and deception and there was nothing I could do.

My dad went into a week-long tirade about my depressed demeanor. I got so sick of hearing that word I considered ripping my ears off.

"Richard, Son, maybe you should try to concentrate on something else, You're too young to be obsessing over a girl. Your depressed demeanor is affecting the whole house."

There was that word again. However, school was on and it was time to get ready. I had no choice but to forget the unfair way life was tossing me around. I simply forced myself to get ready for high school. Mom loved shopping for school clothes. I hated it! Every year we got into a big fight over why I couldn't be with her and not be bratty. Dad kept telling her I was in a funk and had a "depressed demeanor." I was going to ask Lyn to pray for God to take me, but then Marty decided to go school shopping with us.

You might be getting a clue why I started hating Friday. This time it was the only day my mom could take us to the store. Both my folks were in a fit over money, so we started out at K-Mart. Marty decided to walk in backwards so he would look like he's leaving. He said it kept him safe from aliens disguised as K-mart employees.

One of the K-Mart associates only had one tooth and spoke with a weird German accent. I think he had a lisp. Marty went nuts! He swore up and down that this guy used to be one of the kids from our Junior High school that Mrs. Ellie, the yard dog, and her daughter turned into an alien slave. He wouldn't stop. He went on and on until he had me and my mom nuts. We finally had to agree with him to get him to shut up. My mom suggested that all K-Mart employees were aliens.

Marty whispered, "I told you, Richard! You never listen to me." He turned pale and got real quiet.

Our morning at K-Mart had only just begun. One funny little blonde woman in the store had the flu. You could hear her choking and coughing all over the store. Marty wanted to find her and see if she was an ailing alien. Mom didn't want him "running roughshod" all over the store, so he had to stay with us.

Two guys got into an argument and ended up getting escorted out. One of the K-Mart employees walked up while my mom was in the bathroom and said, in some kind of wild alien voice, "Can I help you, or eat your intestines?" Marty bolted. I didn't see him for the rest of the weekend. So there I was, stuck with my mother in K-Mart on a Friday afternoon.

If trying on clothes isn't bad enough, try doing it with your mother shouting through the door, "How do those look Richard?" She wanted me to try on some new pants. I pleaded with her, but she insisted. "I don't want to bring a bunch of clothes back to the return line, Mister!" I knew when she called me or my dad "Mister" there was no use in arguing.

I took the pants into the dressing room and started undressing. I could hear female voices, but I wasn't really paying much attention. I got my pants off and started to try on the new pair. I slipped into the right leg first but my toe got stuck in them before I could get them all the way up. I started jumping in circles and trying to pull the leg on but I lost my balance. My head shot forward, face first, and went right through the flimsy wall into the next dressing room! I looked up and there was Colleen Drew, a girl I knew from school, standing there in her underwear! I just looked at her. There was no way I was going to think of something to say.

Just then, my mom said, "How do those look, Richard?!" I jumped and fell backwards onto my butt.

I pulled the pants on as Colleen yelled, "Mom! Richard Allen is looking at me!"

It took half an hour to convince the store clerk and Colleen's mom that it was an accident. The nightmare ended that night at home when I realized all I ended up with after seven grueling hours at the store was one pair of pants and two blue shirts. My dad thought the whole thing was wildly funny. He never seemed to be on my side. I always thought that if Mom was gone and people were telling lies about him he might see my side better. But I was alone and the world was out to get me.

The first day of school was so crazy it's beyond description. Freshmen are "hog soup" Marty kept saying, last on the bottom end of the social list and first in the target zone. We pushed, shoved, and fought our way to every class. Then an extraordinary event happened that would affect our lives in a big way. Marty and I were waiting for the class before ours to let out so we could go in. Just then, Marty looked up and said, "Hey, look who's comin'!"

I looked over and up came Mark Diverge. Shlock Jock Supreme! He was our number one nemesis all through junior high, and now here he was, about to start in on us the first day of our freshman year. "Hey guys! Pretty rough here, huh?" Then he smiled at Marty and said, "Where's the potato gun?"

His grin was infectious. I was stunned. Marty developed an instant rapport with him and soon, incredibly, we were all fast friends. Thus started a threesome that would last for a very long time. I was blown away at how Marty and Mark worked together. Mark was so funny with his dry wit, it would take me all day sometimes to get his jokes. He was the perfect foil for Marty. One time Mark found a model of a skull in the science class. It was mounted on a stand that was sort of a half orb and rubber-like.

He showed it to Marty, and Marty went wild. He put it on his head, pulled his jacket up over the stand and buttoned it up all the way so the skull stayed on his head.

Mark had a knit cap and some sunglasses in his locker, so he got those and put them on the skull. I was already in our English class when Marty walked in with this absurd costume on. Mark walked in a little behind him. Marty walked over and sat in the desk next to me. The teacher was Mr. Miller, who was the coolest teacher in school. For whatever reason, he decided to ignore the whole weird scene. It was all I could do to keep from losing myself to wild laughter until….

Mr. Miller starts calling out names for the attendance. When he gets to Marty's name, Marty says "Here!" through his buttoned down jacket over his head holding up the skull wearing a knit cap and sunglasses. It was all I could take! I laughed so hard I almost fell out of my seat. Mark had a way of detaching himself and keeping a straight face. I had no such talent. Mr. Miller says, "Richard, are you OK?"

I couldn't answer, I was laughing so hard at the idiot next to me. Mr. Miller told me if I couldn't control myself I'd have to go stand outside the classroom. I gained control and got hold of myself until Mr. Miller said, "OK, today we are going to discuss the Harlequin book I assigned you called, *'Lady, That's My Skull,'* by Carl Shannon." I folded it in, became unglued, and nearly fell out of my seat. Mr. Miller made me leave the room.

After class let out, I had to go in and get a lecture from Miller about not encouraging Marty Shale. His theory was, if you ignored Marty, he would stop behaving that way. What's really insane is, Marty left the class, with everyone else, wearing that stupid thing on his head!

There were many times when someone else would take the heat for Marty. Most of the time it was me. I don't know how he got away with it. Marty and Mark had other things about them, but it would take me a while to learn. Both my friends were wonderfully talented. As the school year wore on, I found out a lot about both of them.

The novelty of school beginning wore off pretty fast for Marty. He started getting into trouble for asking questions in history class. At first the teacher, Mr. Toop, thought Marty's inquisitive nature just needed some constructive direction. It didn't take him long to figure out Marty was being "a smug wise guy," and his questions were designed to amuse me and Mark. Marty didn't really care what the answer was. It got really weird when we were assigned to recite something and Marty got one of Churchill's speeches.

When the day came and Marty was called on to do his part, he flatly refused. Mr. Toop told him it was required. So Marty got up and walked out of the class. Everyone just sat there. Darla Wenton snitted, "Good riddance, Freak," as Marty walked out.

Marty was being slammed hard by his own father. Sam had started beating up Marty's mom pretty badly. Both his parents were drinking. His sister was long gone. Marty's sister had "jumped ship," as Marty put it, just before school started. Aunt Myrtle tried to keep most of it away from him, but Marty was hip to the whole sordid affair. I knew he was angry, but I didn't know where his whole world really was until I went to his house one night. Aunt Myrtle answered the door just as I arrived.

"Come in, Richard, and see poor Marty, He's shot down and so moody."

I went into the dining room where Marty was lying on the floor making paper airplanes. "Mr. Toop said he hopes you never walk through the door of his classroom again!" I said, standing over Marty. I looked down over his occupation.

"I'm not going back there!" he sniffed, and threw an airplane across the room. It went pretty far.

As I watched its flight across the room I said, "Hey, you never showed me your room. Let's go to your room and..." I never got to finish.

Marty interrupted. "You're not going into my room, Dude!"

I hesitated. "Well, maybe I could go into the den and sit there."

As I made my way to the den, Marty jumped up and grabbed me. "No!" he yelled.

Aunt Myrtle heard him and came into the room. "Marty, what is going on?" she said.

"I don't want him getting into my stuff!" he yelled.

Marty's anger seemed way over the top. His aunt got a weird look in her eyes. She wasn't given to anger, but this time Marty pushed too hard. She walked up to Marty and said, "Your option to talking to me that way is either slow or brutal. It could be both." Her eyes squinted as she spoke. It was a face-off. Marty stood firm as they stared at each other, but Myrtle had more experience. Finally, she reached over and pinched Marty.

"OUCH! Crap, man, that hurt!" he hollered.

"Don't you talk like that in this house, Buster Dude O' Boy!" she shot back. "Come with me, Richard."

She waved me over to the den. I felt like I was betraying Marty, but curiosity overcame my sense of loyalty. We walked into the den and I stood there in silent awe. I looked all around at frame after frame of the most beautiful art I'd ever seen! Mind-boggling sketches, watercolors, and some pastels that stunned me. "What is this?" I said to Myrt.

"It's Marty's art work," she said. I turned and stared at Marty. My mouth hung open as I looked at him.

"Marty! I should kill you right now!" I yelled. "What's in your room, Man? Show me now Marty, or I swear I will never speak to you again!" We stood silent just long enough to tick me off even more. "NOW!" I think I scared Marty. He looked at his aunt then looked back at me.

"OK, Rich." He surrendered and we went to his room. I walked into an art gallery filled with sketches of the most incredible description. No words were there, no words were needed. I actually got tears in my eyes.

"I told you, Marty." his aunt said.

I turned and looked at the biggest smart mouth in five states. "Why are you keeping this a secret, Marty?"

Marty's eyes glazed over with deep sadness. He hung his head for a second, then looked at me and said, "My dad says art is for fags." A tear ran down his face. "All the art I drew at home, he destroyed."

I stood there, frozen in a swirling storm of anger and sadness. I don't know where the sudden display of maturity came from, maybe from the art that surrounded me.

"Marty," I said, "He's wrong. I won't say anything bad about him 'cause he's your dad, but he's wrong Marty." We stood and looked at each other for a while. I swear, I don't know how I know this, but both of us grew up at that very moment. "You're going to show this to the world, and I mean it!" I said.

He looked at his aunt in awkward silence. "I'm scared to do that," he said. "What if...?"

His aunt broke in with more love and affection than I ever heard anyone show him and said, "I won't let anyone hurt you, Sweetheart. You can count on that."

I sat on Marty's bed and looked around. Then my eye caught a sketch. "I don't believe you, Man!" I laughed. He came over and smiled.

"Remember eighth grade graduation?" We both laughed. Marty had drawn a picture of the wind blowing my graduation gown up and did an incredible job of capturing the essence of my butt. "Well Man, I hope there aren't too many that will see that!"

"Just everybody!" He howled. All of a sudden, he jumped up and said, "I made something for you. I've been saving it. I'm not sure why." He reached behind his bed and pulled out a large plastic frame, then turned it around. I stared silent and still. It was a picture of Wendy walking across the quad at our junior high.

"Marty, is this mine?"

"Not yet," he replied.

"When?" I asked.

"When it's time, Bro', when it's time." He put it back behind the bed and smiled.

I looked at the clock and said, "We are not done here, but I have homework and I'll see you soon enough." I ran out of the house and down the street. Marty's artwork was racing through my brain, but my heart was bent on Wendy.

Chapter 4

SUNDAY WITH CHAMPIONS

Meeting Mark's family was overwhelming. He had three brothers, all of them big guys. His mom was beautiful! I couldn't peel my eyes off her. I think she was used to men looking at her or something 'cause she would look at me and wink. Mark's dad was a big, half Samoan man, all kind of big, dark, and happy. He laughed a lot and talked about his "champion" who, I finally figured out, was Mark. He loved Mark so much, you could see it in his face. Oddly, I felt a strain around the room.

It was Mark's oldest brother, who couldn't read. He had some brand of learning disability. I soon learned about the tension between them but for now? I couldn't help but compare. Mark and his dad were almost like best friends. I felt distant and confused by my dad. I was in the same place now that I was when Marty asked me what my dad was like - clear back in junior high school.

I didn't know it that day, but having dinner at Mark's house on the first Sunday of every month was going to be a tradition that would last for a long time. Mark's dad slept, ate, and breathed football so the dreams that made him breathe rested right on Mark's shoulders. But the hurt rested on his oldest brother, Michael. I was soon to find out why. Mark's dad kept going on during dinner about the coach advancing Mark from junior varsity to varsity in his freshman year. Finally I asked, "What does that mean?"

"It means 'Golden Boy' is everyone's hero," Michael butted in.

Mark looked stabbed and started to talk back but his mom stepped in. "Not now boys."

"It means Mark is going to play varsity football right away, and the colleges will send out scouts even sooner," his dad said.

"Don't push too hard, Max!" Mark's mom always evened things out.

"I'm just saying the kid's a natural, that's all," his dad said. Then he leaned into me and whispered, "Shawni looks out for Michael."

"Shawni" was Mark's mom's name. So the introduction to Mark's family went. All in all, it was a good time for everyone but Michael, who was hurt inside and would let it out every now and then. Mark and Michael didn't really get along and it showed. Marty and I walked back to his house later that night. We talked about Mark and Michael, then the talk turned for the first time in a long time to Marty's family. Marty told me what was going on with his mom and dad.

"My old man got another DUI. It's his second one in a year. He's drunk all the time. I guess he'll just keel over one of these days. My mom came to see me the day before yesterday. She had a black eye and there were marks on her throat. Myrtle went nuts. My sister is gone, no one knows where." As I listened, it kind of came to me that Marty was pretty unemotional about all of it. He was just sort of stating facts.

"Does any of this make you think about anything?" I asked.

"Yeah, I thank God for 'Myrt the Squirt' every day. She's my mother and father. You and Mark are my two cool brothers. Between Myrt, you, and Mark, I have a family. That's how I think. I have to. I can't let Aunt Myrtle down."

He didn't, either. As the year went on, Marty came home with three trophies. All of them from art contests. He ended up with five thousand bucks!

Spring break was on. I spent the weekend helping my dad clean the garage. Marty and Mark went to hang out at the mall. I wanted to go, but Dad needed me, and I was angry at life. I didn't bother trying to bring anything up. I already knew what my dad's answer was anyway. By Sunday evening, I was so tired I couldn't think.

The garage was full of junk no one could have ever wanted or needed. But there it was, taking up space. I finally got the "All through!" from Dad and went to my room. No sooner did I flop than I heard Mark and Marty coming down the hall.

"Hey, wake up! Man, you're gonna flip!" Marty blasted into the room followed by Mark. Both of them had big smiles.

"We take care of our own," Mark laughed. Then Marty reached into his pocket and pulled out an envelope. It was a letter from Wendy's mom from her Aunt Rachel.

"How did you get this?" I said.

"We were at the mall and Marty saw Wendy's aunt getting out of her car," Mark replied.

"How did you know it was her?

"She was with a little kid, he was eating a donut." Marty laughed.

Mark's eyes glowed as he told the story. "They headed across the parking lot and went into the mall so we went over to investigate. It was open and there was this letter inside. It was addressed to Rachel from Texas! I kept lookout while Marty reached in and grabbed it! Then guess what we did?"

"I don't know." I said.

"We ran, Man!" Marty and Mark started laughing and high-fiving all over my room. I looked at the letter...

"I have to read this by myself," I said.

"We pillaged and burned for you, Bro'." Mark's voice was slow and quiet.

"This means so much to me, but I have to read it by myself," I said, as seriously as I could. We withstood the silence as long as possible, then we all started laughing. "Come on you guys, I'll be out there in a while." They left the room while I took the letter out of the envelope. It was long, so I sat in my chair and started reading.

"Dear Rachel,

I know this is going to affect you adversely, but I've finally gotten some good news. As you know, losing my job was a hardship I never counted on. Danny was only three when Tom was killed in Viet Nam. He hardly remembers his own father. Wendy was five and still talks about her daddy and how much she loved him. Getting fired because Robert Sallis couldn't keep his hands to himself was sickening. He used his power and influence to get rid of me.

I just heard from Cathy Ingals. She's head of the sales division now. Robert was fired after one of the women there brought a sexual harassment suit against him. I left the job I had in Colorado for a year-long training program in Houston. I want Wendy to finish school and summer to get here before we move again. Then we will be back for good. I feel so sorry for Wendy. She is sullen and withdrawn at times, I know she must blame me for taking her away from her friends and home. Thanks for sending Wendy Carl's address. I will remind her to write to him.

Your impression of Richard Allen worries me. Do you think he will try to get to Wendy when we return? I don't like being over-occupied with this, but his mother has always been so nice. You know, I also have Danny to consider. He's a teenager now. I don't know what to do with a teenage boy. The trip to Houston was awful. It started to rain as we got into Texas and I took a wrong turn. It took me all day to find my way back. The kids were good, but all of us got so frustrated.

Traveling by car is arduous at best. Going from state to state with two kids and a load of luggage is backbreaking and heart-rending. God, I wish Tom was here to help me! I miss him so much, sometimes I just sit and cry. But the training is going well, and like I said, we will all be back as soon as my training is complete. Wendy is ready for the last year of school. Do you believe that?

She is such a beautiful girl. I love her so much. I just worry if her priorities are all right. She still wants to dance and I think she's trying to get hold of Richard. You have such a bad view of him, but he has really good parents. How could he be that bad? Wendy has been forbidden to contact him, but I think she tries anyway. Remember how Mom went off when she first met Tom? Oh brother, the more she despised him the more I loved him. You know how that goes. Wendy may have sent a letter to Richard through Carl Simms, but I sure don't know if he got it. Danny says he can't wait to get back home. I guess I can't either. Having a female boss might go a little better after what I've been through.

I have to relate a strange coincidence. After we got settled in Houston, I decided to take the kids out for dinner. There was a band at the place where we ate and Wendy recognized one of the musicians. She got his attention during a break. His name is Lance Cawlngs. His band is really good! They play country swing. Good lord, that kid can play a guitar!

Anyway, he was in high school when Wendy was in Jr. high and she remembered him playing at the dances. He remembered a lot of the kids she knew. It was so cute! When dinner was over, Wendy went over and said Goodnight to him. He was so kind to her. I guess his father was killed some years ago in Memphis.

Anyway, I know you're having a hard time with Scooter. I think once he starts on his med's he will be fine. I hope and believe I've given you more than enough warning. We will be back in little over a year. I'm sorry I have to write, but there is so much information and I'm in such a hurry all the time, it seems better to just write it all down. See ya soon! Love, Sis."

I couldn't believe what I read. Carl Sims was being pushed at Wendy while I was being lied about. It also sounded like Wendy was trying to get through to me. I knew what I had to do! There just comes a time in every man's life when he has to take the bull by the tail and face the situation. I put the letter back in the envelope, put it in my back pocket, and headed for the door. I'm not sure where Mark and Marty were, but I was on a mission and I didn't have time to waste.

I walked the two miles over to the street where Wendy's aunt lived in her mom's house. I knew Carl Sims lived somewhere nearby. The whole way I kept thinking that Marty and Mark were behind me, but every time I looked back, they weren't there. I walked up the street where Wendy lived, now the home of her wretched, wrong-headed aunt. I saw Carl Simms coming the other way on his skateboard. He saw me and stopped. I walked deliberately toward him like I saw the cowboys do in the movies my grandpa always watched.

"Hey Allen, you better not try anything," he said as I got closer. I grabbed his collar and pulled it as tight as I could.

"Where are the letters Wendy sent me? Tell me or I'll really… do something!" OK, it wasn't as cool as the threats gunslingers make, but they have writers. I don't.

His face was red but he was able to croak out, "Wendy's aunt has them. I got to know her 'cause I babysit for her sometimes when she needs to go out and run errands."

"You watch that kid of hers?" I asked, about as perplexed as I could be.

"Yeah she told me what you did to Scooter at the mall. Anyway I told her how me and Wendy sometimes did stuff like hang out and that Wendy was sending me letters to smuggle to you."

"Where are they?" I shouted in his face. I let him go, just enough so he could tell me she kept them in a jar in the pantry of her kitchen.

"She pays me two dollars each to give them to her instead of bringing them to you."

"If you ever tell anyone about this, so help me, I will find you and beat you to a bloody nugget." My voice sounded hoarse and threatening, or so I hoped. I walked away feeling shaky and scared of myself. I never did anything like that before. It also gave me the confidence to head straight to Wendy's house. I knocked on the door as hard as I could.

"I'd rethink this part of the plan if I were you." A voice from behind me spoke. I turned around expecting to see Mark or Marty. What I saw was a policeman. "Come along Son, I think you need a ride home."

I will never forget the look on Mom's face when a cop car pulled up with me in the back seat. The cop explained he had seen me starting a fight with a kid a couple of miles from here and he thought it might be best to just bring me back home where I could cool my "spurs." His cowboy analogy amused me and I laughed. "You know, young man, I could have taken you to the juvenile facility downtown," he said. This made me wonder if knocking on a door was some violation of the law, but I didn't say anything.

"Richard, this is not funny!" Mom was not to be reckoned with. Then I saw my dad.

"Richard Allen, if this has anything to do with that girl I'm going to ground you for the summer!" Dad was on Mom's side and I was doomed. The policeman left. I was there with my mom, my dad, and both my sisters. "What did you do 'Twitchy Richie?' Start an idiot riot?" Samantha said.

My dad walked over to Samantha and stared her into silence, and then into leaving the room. "I can't ever participate in the good stuff," she moaned as she left the room.

My little sister Lyn stood there wiping tears from her eyes. "Just look at what you've done to our family!" She yelled, and then went sweeping into her room.

Mom rolled her eyes and turned her glare on me. "Start talking, Dude."

Her demeanor was threatening, but she stayed calm for the time being. I stood in silent protest to the outworking of a situation that should have been resolved long ago. I felt a hot breath on my neck and looked to my left. My dad was an inch from my face.

"Start talking or I will put you on work restriction for the rest of the year!" he hissed. I stood there quietly waiting for the sting of parental justice. Both of them sat down and looked at me.

Then Mom said, "We're ready when you are, and we can wait."

It was a standoff of epic proportions! They sat there and I stood there. So it went. They sat and I stood. The policeman brought me home at 7 PM. The standoff started at about 7:30, and it was now 9:30 My sister Samantha grabbed her car keys and split after hour one. Lyn came out of her room once and read a prayer she had written.

"Dear God, My brother Richard is in lots of trouble. If you don't intervene it will get to be double. How this will end no one can tell, but if you don't help Richard, he's going to hell."

My mom said, "That's nice, Honey, but now you have to let us talk to Richard. He's being a big snoot and I'm about out of rope."

Without thinking I snorted. "Your rope is short and unfair."

She came over and said, "I'm giving you one last chance, Mister. Then I'm going to turn you over to your dad. I won't see your pain. I won't hear your cries for help. I won't notice your pleading. Talk now, or I walk out, and when I do, you're all his."

"I love Wendy." I whispered.

"I knew it!" My dad said.

"What did you do Richard? Tell me." Mom's voice was softer.

"I threatened Carl Simms!" I said, loud and proud. "I should have beaten him blue!" I yelled. "But I let him off the hook for talking."

"Carl Simms?" Dad said.

"Yes! I think I might kick his ass tomorrow too!"

"Go to your room, Mister!" Mom said, giving me a little push on the shoulder. I wasn't sure why I said the thing about whippin' up on Carl tomorrow. I had no intention of anything like that. I guess I was tired and angry.

As I lay on my bed, I could hear them talking in low whispers from my dad's office. Then Dad's phone rang. He picked up before the answering machine got it. The call lasted for about half an hour. Then a sort of "Quiet before the storm" set in.

Another half hour ticked slowly by. He called my name. "Richard! In here, now!" I went into the den and stood there. He sat down on his chair and said, "That was Ed Simms. He *was* a client of mine. You know, Simmmssss? As in 'Carl?' He decided to change brokers! Do you know why? Well, let me tell you, tough guy. It's because of your antics. That's why I lost a client. We've already been having enough money problems and now you made them worse. Tell me Richard, what is wrong with you? Tell me why I lost a client?"

"Well Dad, I guess that's the way the cookie crumbles." I said.

It didn't have the effect I thought it would. It didn't show him that when something was important to me, it's what *he* said. I just watched his face crumble into hurt and disappointment. It didn't make me feel vindicated either. I just stood there in the silence and watched my dad struggle with more money problems and a client lost because of me.

"I don't want you in my office anymore!" he said. So I left. Into my room I went. I shut the door, and that was that.

"What's your dad like?" That's what Marty asked me way back in eighth grade. I still didn't have an answer. I do know this: The feeling in our home changed after that. It would be some time before there was anything like closeness or kinship between me and my father. Even Mom wasn't quite the same for a while. Her real estate company was in a slump. She hadn't sold anything for some time. My dad complained about the long lines at the gas station. Mom was always going on about "stagflation" and the oil crisis. Samantha started staying away more, and Lyn just sort of kept to herself with her pet rocks that she named and talked to. There wasn't enough money in the first place, and I just made it worse. I was mega-grounded. I knew better than to ask if I could go anywhere.

Spring break ended and summer was coming on. I talked enough to Mark and Marty to let them know not to bother. My name was "Mr. Black Sheep Mudface" in this family, and it would be awhile before I even got "I guess you're still our son" status. The one thing that helped was reading. I read everything. Mostly books about lonely dreamers like Don Quixote. I liked science fiction, so I read a lot of that.

By the time I hit sixteen, I was into Jack Kerouac. I read *On The Road* about ten times. My sister Samantha came into my room once and was trying to talk me into giving her ten dollars. She was sniffing around looking for something to implicate me so she could blackmail me, when all of a sudden she ripped my mattress up and looked under it.

"Holy crud Richard! Most guys your age have girly mags under their bed. You have *On the Road* by Jack who's-his-what's-it."

"That's 'Kerouac!'" I said.

"Why is it under here little brother? Is it 'cause dad doesn't want you reading this?" she said, knowing full well she had all the low down on me she needed to get what she wanted. She made soft eyes and said, "Come on, Sweetheart, I really need your help this time."

I dug up change out of my water jar that served as a change wasteland and gave her eight dollars and fifty cents.

"That's it," I told her. Now you have to stop listening to The Ramones and unless you want a ton of pennies, that's It!" "Thank you, Richard. You saved my life. Now that I know The Ramones bother you, I'll play it louder." she said, smiling as she left the room.

Years later, I learned that she had owed money on a parking ticket. By then, it was too late to get her back.

It was slow, but finally summer came. My parents always took us out for dinner when school ended, but not this year. I wasn't sure if it was because of me, or if they just didn't have enough money. Anyway, Lyn got it into her head that it was my fault, and she decided to confront me.

"I'm sure you understand by now what sadness you've heaped on this melancholy tribe. So now it's time to apologize and humbly beg Mom and Dad to take us to our End-of-the-School Year dinner. If you can't do it for yourself, do it for me."

"Why should I do it for you?" I asked.

"'Cause every year I get fried shrimp and I was really looking forward to my fried shrimp." Her look was innocent but firm.

"You don't understand, little Sister, I'm fighting for love and love is what men die for."

"Why can't you be into disco and roller skating like all the other lost souls in this world?" she said.

"Lyn!" Came my mom's voice as she made her way down the hall. "Lyn, I just got the info on summer camp and I wanted to look it over with you." She entered the room and stood there waiting for Lyn's response.

"I'm not going to camp this year, I'm not going until Richard apologizes."

Mom looked at me and said, "Is this what it's come to? Now you're indoctrinating your lovely little sister into your rebellion?"

NOTE: SUMMER CAMP? BUT THEY CAN'T AFFORD DINNER?

"Go away!" I hollered. Just then, Dad came in, got Lyn and Mom, and ushered them out, closing the door. All without a word.

"And stay out!" I yelled. I was going to have to realize many times, if you keep your mouth shut, things go a lot smoother. I hadn't learned that just yet.

My dad got so mad he contacted Mr. Diverge and had him set me up to join Mark in football camp.

"I'm not going to 'football' anything," I told him.

"I'm going to drive you there and I'm going to bring you home," he shot back. Samantha was in her room, doing homework, and heard all of it.

"Richard the Jock Strap!" She called from the other room. Mom walked over and closed her door.

"You know, Richard, you brought this on yourself," she told me.

"Camp starts next week, Buddy. I suggest you get ready." Dad was not taking "No" for an answer.

I stayed in my room as mad and outraged as I could get. "I'm not going to any jock camp!" I yelled through the door. Something had to be done. Wendy was in Houston. Her aunt was telling lies about me and my parents were only interested in their rules and regulations.

I couldn't take any more. I sat and thought it all over giving each part of the situation as much consideration as I could. I thought about Don Quixote, Jack Kerouac, and Huckleberry Finn. Then it came to me. I knew what had to be done. I had the right idea. I just didn't take it far enough. If Wendy was in Houston, then that's where I should be! I jumped off the bed and started digging through the closet. I found an old bag with a handle on it and a nice, long strap. I loaded some of my clothes into it and laid on my bed 'till midnight. I was so sure of myself. How could I let this stuff just roll over me? If no one was going to help me, I'd help myself.

I wondered what it was going to be like when morning came and I wasn't there. They'd probably go on just like always. They might even be glad not to have so many kids in the house. Midnight came. All was quiet. I revisited my reasoning and all of it was sound and logical! I wanted to clear my name, and I wanted to be with Wendy. I checked the things in my bag, got ten bucks from my change jar, went to the window, and slid it open. I stepped up from my desk chair, lifted the screen out and eased myself out the window.

The air was cold. It was a clear night. There were still lots of sounds, but mostly my footsteps. I went down the street, around the corner, and up to the main road that went to the highway. I was sure I would reach my goal in a day or two. The cars moaned past, then slipped away.

Some turned, some kept going, until the sound of them slowly faded. I thought about Lyn and how she would pray. Samantha might go looking for me, but grumble about it the whole time. My parents would worry a little at first, but get used to the fact that I was out on my own. "On my *own*." That sounded just about right. The night was ready for me and so was the road. I made it to the freeway around 1 AM. I was excited, free, and away from any distractions that might keep me from my goal. No one was going to stop me now! I was on my way to Houston.

Chapter 5

ARE YOU KIDDING?!

I Remember Dad telling people, when he gave directions to the freeway, that it was about three miles away. By the time I got there, it was past AM. There was a gas station mini-mart down the road near the on-ramp. Just before I got there, I stopped and bought a hot dog and a soda. It got colder and colder as the night wore on. I was sure that just standing there with my thumb out right by the on-ramp would get me to Houston in no time. By five in the morning, I was getting pretty tired. I thought I should sleep or at least rest awhile.

I went back to the mini-mart and slipped in behind the dumpster. The smell almost killed me. There were big globes of sickening looking whatever on the ground. The dumpster was full of old oil cans that were falling out over the top. Half eaten hot dogs and boxes with slimy bog, other boxes stuffed inside them added to the mess. I sat down in the least gross spot I could find and tried to close my eyes. The sound of traffic was unending. Voices at the station, horns blasting, semi-trucks grinding through their gears assaulted my nerves. Once, a cup half full of ice came over the wall and landed on my face. Sleep was out of the question.

I dragged myself back to the on-ramp and stuck out my thumb. By this time, the sun was up and there were cars going in every direction. I began to realize I was going about this all wrong. How can anyone pick me up if they don't know where I'm going? I hustled back to the mini-mart. Slipped in behind the dumpster and tore a piece of cardboard from a box. I had to ask people who were busy pumping gas if any one of them had a marker. One guy told me to "Mark this!" and an old lady asked me to drive her to Barstow. It took two hours to finally find someone who had a marker and allowed me to use it.

The marker came from a girl who made me pump her gas for the loan of her marker. I finally had a piece of cardboard with "Houston" in bold black letters on it. I went back to the on-ramp, held up my sign, and waited. Around noon, I went back to the mini-mart and got a small bag of peanuts and a bottle of water. I took some time to finish off my snack before I went back to the on-ramp. I held high my cardboard sign for all the cars passing by to see. I had a destination.

I waved, I smiled, and I pointed at the sign. I stood looking cool, I tried looking hip. I sat down and held out the sign. The time went by fast. I got so tired I started to drift to sleep on my feet. I went back to the mini-mart and sat down behind the dumpster. After about an hour I went in, used the bathroom, bought a bag of jerky, and went back to the on-ramp.

As evening came on, the traffic got super thick. Only they were all going the other direction. "Maybe there's more than one Houston," I thought. People are confused 'cause they don't know which Houston I'm going to. I went back to the mini-mart and started asking people if they had a marker I could use. One nice lady had a pencil, so I used that. Back at the on-ramp I held up my sign until it got too dark to see. Maybe they will see my sign with their headlights. By ten PM I was dead on my feet. I went back to the mini-mart and returned to my spot behind the dumpster. Only this time someone was there.

An old man was sitting there on a bucket turned upside down. His bare feet were calloused and dirty. His pants, worn and sewn with some mismatched string, hung loosely on his hips. He had more than one shirt on, and the holes in one showed through to the holes in the other. His thin frame was topped off by a face, care and weather-worn. It hid what once must have been a young face just like mine. He looked up, then looked away. He tried to hide his feet then looked up again. "I seen ya for a while now, holdin' up yer sign." He spoke in a gravelly whisper.

"No one wants to give me a ride." I said.

He coughed, then laughed. "Hell, Son, yer not gonna git a ride from anyone, they don't even know yer there."

"I just want to get to Houston."

"Houston!" He yelled. "Hell, I'm from Houston. Got drafted when I was 18. Ain't been home since."

"Why haven't you been home?"

"It's no use. The world is ugly. Tore my soul outta me. Three tours In 'Nam. I seen stuff that no one should see. My younger brother lost his legs over there. He's lucky. They sent me back home, nobody wanted me. Not any of us!

Not anyone. I couldn't sleep or eat. I screamed at night. Hell, my folks had their hands full taking care of Robert." He looked at me and almost smiled.

"The name's Jimmy Doolan. I like to know who I'm talkin' to."

"I'm Richard Allen You were in the war in Southeast Asia?"

He looked at me cock-eyed and said, "Where'd ya hear that?"

"In school, we had to watch old news reports aboutViet Nam."

"I saw Eric Lowes layin' on the ground, arm shot off, cryin' for his mommy." Jimmy started crying and begging God to forgive him. "It's all my fault," he kept saying. He dug into his jacket and pulled out a hand-rolled cigarette and lit it. He handed it over to me.

I said, "No, I don't smoke." I could tell by the smell of it that it wasn't tobacco.

"I been eatin' outta garbage cans so long I forgot what real food tastes like. Now, why are ya runnin' off to Texas, Son?"

I reached into my pocket, pulled out the remaining $4.25, and handed it to him. "I can't remember, Mr. Doolan, but I think you need this more than I do."

I lifted myself up, turned, and left the dumpster. I heard him cough as he kept right on talking. I don't know if he knew I had left him or not.

There was a bus stop near the corner of the mini-mart, so I sat there and waited. I think the bus came and went a few times while I sat there. I can't be sure.

The fact was, no one was going to give me a ride anywhere. It was a whole day since I left and I hadn't even gotten out of my own neighborhood. That poor man over there behind the dumpster left home when he was 18. He saw friends get killed and wounded. He saw death all around him. He never went home. He couldn't. He didn't know how. I was mad 'cause I couldn't see or talk to Wendy. I was sad. I felt angry at myself, angry at the world.

As I sat there, the wind started blowing and it got even colder. I must have sat there for some time, 'cause it started getting light again. Then it started to get all misty. I hadn't even noticed the clouds. I sat and stared. My sign got wet and fell apart. My clothes got soaked. No one came to see about me, or ask what I was doing there. Life just kept on going. The traffic got thick then settled back down. There were sounds of cars everywhere. That's why I never noticed when my dad pulled up. He came over and sat down beside me. I looked up at him and burst into tears.

He put his arm around me and said, "I ran away from home when I was 12. I went to join the circus. I actually found one and tried to get the man to hire me. He started hitting me with a riding crop. He beat me right off the circus grounds. It sounds cruel, but I think he knew it was the best thing for me. At least that's what I'd like to believe."

I sat there with my old man in the mist on that bus bench for some time. Struck with a whole day and just one night of dealing with the real world. "Dad, how come Jack Kerouac and all those guys could hitch-hike all over the place?"

"Richard, Jack Kerouac was a writer. He wrote *On The Road* on a large paper roll. Do you think he ran all over the country with a big roll of paper under his arm writing down his adventures? All those beat poets and writers were young and starting their work during the

1950's. Coffee was a nickel then. There was enough money and things were calm enough for those guys to run around bragging about their Bohemian life-styles. The very people they put down were the very ones that paid for them to do what they did." He looked down at the duffle bag with my clothes in it and said, "While we're at it, how did you find my tote-bag from college?"

"That's Rocinante," I answered.

"You named my tote-bag after Don Quixote's horse?"

"Yes."

"Ok, well maybe we can revisit that later. Your mother is so upset and sick with worry she hasn't slept since you left and there's more news, Your grandpa got wind of you running away and he wants to see you.

"Dad, is he going to make me watch "How The West Was Won?"

"I don't think so Son, I think he just wants to talk to you. He's old, Richard, maybe you can learn something from him."

"Do I have to?"

"Look, it will help me ease you back into the house. Your mom was out of her mind with worry."

My dad spoke softly but matter of fact. "Lyn is praying that God will bring you home safe, and for the life of me I can't understand anything Samantha does." He looked at me and said, "I'll bet you're hungry."

"Kinda. Peanuts and a drink was all I could come up with."

"I'll tell you what, Richard, I will tell your mom that you're safe and sound. And then you and I will go get a nice breakfast. Then I'll take you to see your grandpa. How's that sound?"

"All right," I said.

With that, we went to the car and drove away. I will never see a dumpster the same way again. I will never see a homeless person the same way again, I will call to mind how Jimmy Doolan looked many times throughout my life. We went around the mini-mart and passed the dumpster. I could still hear Jimmy singing and talking to himself. This would stay with me forever.

After breakfast, Dad took me to see my grandpa.

Dad had some business and errands to do and said he would pick me up later. I went up the walk. The door opened without me knocking. My grandpa stood there and looked at me.

"I heard you ran off! Is that right?"

"Yes." I didn't mean to be short of words, but I was tired and a little flustered at almost everything.

He looked at me for a while then said, "Sit down sweet Boy."

He sat in his big wing-back chair that was aimed at the T.V. with two very old doilies my grandma made on the arms of his chair. There were all of his things surrounding the chair. A coffee cup, His ashtray, a newspaper. A small radio, and a pack of Camel unfiltered cigarettes. He grabbed the pack of Camels and took one out. I watched him light it and pull his ashtray around for easy reach. He took a puff and looked at me again. Then he sort of chuckled to himself.

"I ran off when I was seventeen. Never looked back. Met your grandmother at a dance. I always hated those dances, but it was a good place to meet girls. When her folks found out we were spendin' lots of time together they lost their lunch, so to speak. They told your grandma to stop flirtin' with poor white trash like me. It was awful. My daddy was a rag man and mama did ironing for half the town. When Em refused, they packed up kit and caboodle and left for California.

I started to realize that he knew more about me and Wendy than I ever told him. Lyn came over to see him a lot so I guess that's where he got the lowdown on my fight for love.

"What did you do?" I asked.

He took another drag at his smoke then put it out. "I got what I could together, stole five dollars from my dad who was working too much to pay any real attention, and ran off to California. In those days, five dollars was a lot of money. I knew where they were 'cause Emily was able to sneak a letter to me through her cousin Sarah Lyn. I rode trains, hitchhiked, and walked all the way to find her." I was dumbfounded. I thought my grandpa was just an old guy who lived in his house alone or something. I didn't know about how he married my grandmother.

"What happened then, Grandpa? I mean, what did you do?"

"I found their home. I sat and watched them for about three days. Then one day Em came out with a grocery list in one hand and three dollars in the other. I stayed out of sight until she got round the corner then I ran over to her. I said, "Let's hightail it out of here!""

"Holy crud, man! Did you elope?" I asked, startled.

"None of those folks ever saw us again for about twelve years. By that time, your Uncle Danny was born and your mom was on the way." I felt close to him. Closer than I ever knew I could.

I looked at the old man sitting across the room and said, "Grandpa, no one understands."

"They understand more than you know, Richard. Life is hard. Sometimes it's downright crappy. They just don't want you to get hurt or mess up someone else."

"Should me and Wendy elope?" I asked.

"Shoot, no! Those were different times when me and your grandma ran off. You do somethin' like that now and the FBI will hunt you down and make trouble for you for years. Ya can't do romantic things like run off these days."

He looked tired and pretty gray. There came a knock on his door. It was my dad. It was time to go home and face Mom and my sisters. He put his arm around me and patted me on the shoulder. "It's all good Rich," he said as he looked at me. "Lyn told me to say that." He smiled and walked back into his house.

With that, we were headed back home. I never saw my grandpa again. He died three weeks later from a stroke. I would always remember that he fought for love. It gave me greater resolve to fight for what I thought was right. To those who know, it goes without saying, there are some who don't know how good it feels to sleep in your own bed. I knew the difference and would often remember trying to sleep behind a dumpster. I fell fast asleep.

Mom came in, petted my head, and kissed me. Day turned into night and I slept it through. Soon I would have to face the world and the people I ran away from. When I woke up, it all seemed strangely different. It looked the same but it wasn't. There were changes; some good, some not so good. I came out to the living room. Both my sisters were sitting there, talking to Mom and Dad. When I walked into the room, the talk stopped and all of them looked at me

"You caused quite an uproar, little Brother." Sam said.

Mom stood up, came over and hugged me. "Please don't ever do that again." She spoke into my ear.

Then she held my head in her hands and, looking straight into my eyes said, "Please."

"I'm sorry Mom I'm sorry I hurt all of you."

"Well there's been enough drama around here, but I want to tell all of you something." Dad was less emotional. "We almost lost this house. The work is slow and if it weren't for a couple of houses your mom sold, we might very well be moving. I want to ask all three of you to remember something. This is our house. You live here. As long as you do, we will take care of you. We love you and want you to have all that goes with it. But please, keep the crap to a minimum."

He left the room, having said what he needed to say. I was still at a loss, but I'd seen enough and had Mark and Marty to contend with. Mark was easy. He begged me to come to the rest of football camp. "We need a water boy, and it'll be cool having you there, Man! C'mon, please?" I agreed and made the arrangements. Then I went to find Marty. First, I went to his house. Myrtle hugged me for about an hour. At least that's how it seemed. I checked the mall, but he wasn't there. It suddenly dawned on me where he was.

The tree fort had vines all over it. It looked cool. I went up the rope ladder and looked inside. Marty wasn't there. For lack of anything better to do, I went home. When I got back home the house was quiet. I went to my room, intent on reading. I walked in and saw two shoes sticking out from under my bed. Pretending not to notice, I flopped on my bed and started a dialog. Out loud.

"Poor Marty! He'll never know that I was really abducted by bloodthirsty aliens. I won't let on until I have him cornered and I'm about to cast my alien brainwashing spell on him."

"That's not funny, man!" Came a plaintive cry from inside my closet.

"I thought you were under the bed!" I laughed. A sock-clad Marty walked out of the closet.

"Aliens aren't something that normal people joke about!" he yelled.

I started laughing my butt off as he put his shoes back on.

"No! This is all I can stand. First you run off without me. Then you become one of the cursed aliens from Uranus." He slid toward the door with only his toes inside his shoes. Then he turned around and said, "Don't leave me here by myself, EVER." Very seriously. Then he left. I wasn't going to see him again for a while, 'cause first I had football camp. Then something was up that I was totally unaware of. Marty had a girlfriend!

"A what?!" I said to Mark on the way to camp the next morning.

"That's right. Her name is Dagmar!" He smiled as he spoke.

"Dagmar?"

"You heard me the first time, Bro."

I was utterly speechless. I sat there wondering how this came about. So I asked. "How did this come about?"

"She's a painter. She and Marty are always competing in contests. That's where they met, I think, and, well, you know... love finds a way." I was consumed with the idea of Marty with a girl and couldn't wait to see her.

I soon found out, being a water boy has its downside. I mean, "Low man on the totem pole" doesn't even come close. I got knocked down about a thousand times. Guys kept calling me "The Water Butt" and the coach didn't even care! He just kept calling the players "girls" and telling them if they wanted to win a game, they were going to have to play like they wore pants and not dresses.

I kept thinking how great it would be to be at home, finishing *The Three Musketeers*. Camp was all day! It made me sick! What a waste. I was so beat I could hardly walk. I sat down on the bench trying to count the blisters on my feet without removing my shoes when I heard a voice. "Wow! You really got your can kicked!" I looked up, and there was a girl I remembered from eighth grade.

"You're Kate Ridgeway."

I knew I remembered her, but I didn't remember what I was looking at now. She had grown. Her hair was kind of at her shoulders, but seemed longer. She had bright blue eyes, was a little taller than me, and was rather charming.

"What are you doing at football camp?" was all I could think of to say.

"I'm the head of the cheerleader squad. I'm here to see how many girls show up, take their names, and give the list to Coach Harlin."

I couldn't wait to get to camp the rest of the week. Although my talents as a water boy came into question every second, talking to Kate was fun. She said she liked me, and hoped that she and I could go to Homecoming together. This was too good to be true!

I was still glad when camp ended. For whatever reason, it was over on Thursday afternoon. When I got home, I flopped down and said, "Thank God that crap is over."

Lyn and Mom heard me. Then I heard Dad say, "You're in it now." Mom heard him and both of us had to apologize to Lyn.

"Mom, I can't say anything around here, I don't have any first amendment rights."

"It's OK, Mom." Lyn said. All of us turned and looked at her.

"Lyn's a sinner!" I said. Then I jumped up and ran to Marty's house. When I got there, Myrtle was hoeing the garden and told me to go on insides. I walked in and found Marty and Dagmar swapping spit.

"You must be Dagmar," I laughed. "I hope you know what you've gotten yourself into."

"Hey, I've revised my stand on aliens and I know they really exist. Dagmar has shown me the right way to look at it. Now we share a strong belief in the alien counter-culture that lives among us!" Marty said, never taking his eyes off Dagmar. Myrtle told me to make myself at home.

"What's for dinner?" I asked, strolling into the kitchen.

"Dagmar, this is Richard Allen." Marty said, mildly contrite. "He's one of the aliens living among us. So tell us Richie, how far did you get when you ran off to wherever?"

"I got to the on-ramp by the freeway," I whispered.

"Are you kidding? Is that it?!" Marty started howling.

"Man, you could've run away without ever leaving your house! Next time, tell me and we can go nowhere together."

He never let me live it down. But for the time being, we settled in. It was cool having Dagmar there. She was trying to teach him how to do the hustle. Teaching Marty anything was an exercise in insanity.

The rest of that summer wasn't much. Mark talked about football season. Marty and Dagmar battled it out in every art competition they could find. I hung out where I could, and read anything I got my hands on. Sophomore year was boring and uneventful. Junior year started with a thud. My dad was in front of the T.V. watching the Viking II land on Mars. Mom talked about Billy Carter and what a dorf he was. Lyn played Norman Greenbaum's Spirit in the Sky over and over till Sam complained and mom had to step in.

I didn't feel like going to school, but I was really looking forward to seeing Kate. We had two classes together. Mark and I had shop class. Shop classes worked like this: Each quarter you had to pass every variety of shop class. One quarter was auto body, one was drafting, one was electricity class, and the fourth was woodworking. So by the end of the year, you had taken all the different shop classes. We got into electrical class, and it's all guys. There's like, twenty-five sixteen- and seventeen-year-olds all shouting their heads off and acting nuts. I couldn't believe this mess! I wasn't all too enthused about the class in the first place, but this made it even worse. Mark thought it was great. Every Tuesday and Wednesday he would get there early and draw game plans on the whiteboard.

The teacher for this class was Mr. Fisk. I swear, he looked just like Barney from "The Andy Griffith Show." He was thin and nervous, always kind of bossy. So one day one of the guys asked, "Is it possible to run electricity through some kinds of vegetables?"

Mr. Fisk says, "Yes, you can. For instance, a bodado." The whole room froze for a second and all twenty-five dudes in the room busted out laughing! I couldn't believe it! He said, "badado!" Not "potato," but "bodado!" I was dying.

We spent the rest of the quarter asking vegetable questions in electricity class. Mr. Fisk would get mad and yell, "We are NOT talking about BODADOES today!" Then all of us would scream with laughter. Needless to say, none of us got much out of electricity class.

Another Friday from hell was on my horizon. But first, I was escorted by the entire DiVerge family to the Homecoming game at our school. I sat near Mr. DiVerge who explained the game to me as we went along. I had a pretty good understanding from being the water boy at camp. But I didn't want to ruin Mr. D's chance to talk about Mark. I would soon see why he was so proud.

Our team was on the receiving side. First, the ball ended up at about the twenty-six yard line. Mark came out with the offensive unit. They huddled, then clapped their hands and went to line up. I was stunned by what I saw next! When the ball was snapped, Mark faded back and snapped his arm. This made the defense stop for a second. Mr. D called it a "pump fake." Then Mark threw the football. The ball blasted from his hand like a bullet! It just blew across the field! You could hear it smack the receiver right in the chest. The crowd gasped, and then cheered. Throw after throw was elegant and perfect. Mark never missed.

I was so blown away, I couldn't speak. This kid wasn't good. He was great! Now I knew why every college in the country wanted him. Now I knew why they called him "Shotgun." I felt so overshadowed by my friends.

One was a wonderful artist. The other was a great quarterback! I was soon to find a place for myself, but first, life got a bit ugly.

The football game took us to the Homecoming dance. Kate and I had been having a great time together. We made the date, I was looking forward to it. Mom helped me buy a really great shirt and a new pair of black dress pants. I was so excited to go with Kate. I told my sister Samantha all about it.

"Wow Richard aren't' you going behind Wendy's back?" She laughed. I didn't answer. I just shrugged and pretended not to notice.

After the football game we got ready for the dance. Kate called and asked if I would meet her there. The plans were made. Mark already had his driver's license. He was going with a girl named Allison Love. They picked me up at seven and we headed for the gym at school. When we got there, I met Kate and handed her a corsage. She laughed and said, "You're supposed to pin it on me, Silly."

The dance was great and for the first time I was not thinking about Wendy. My mind was on Kate, and all the things I wanted to do with my life.

JUNIOR YEAR??

The rest of our junior year was bland and stuffed with homework. Fall turned to winter. 1977 was on its way. Between classes, you could find me at the library. I buried myself in books. Then, as winter slowly turned into spring, I landed a drafting class. It was separate from the general shop classes and was there for people to pursue drafting. I loved drafting! It was analytical and artistic at the same time. I drowned myself in it. I told my dad that I wanted to be an architect. He liked the idea, and encouraged me along the way.

Spring break was coming on, so Marty, Mark, and I decided to do something like we used to. Just us three. All of us wanted to spend an evening in the city. Mark's dad had a friend who owned a big place where you could eat, drink, play video games, shoot pool, and hang out. All of us jumped at the idea and so came another turning point in my life from a most unexpected source.

Chapter 6

YOU DID!

The evening was upon us. We piled into Mark's dad's car and drove out for a guys' night on the town. We had a ball! Myrtle gave Marty a wad of money. I robbed my savings. Mark had won a bet with his dad about throwing three touchdowns in a row. So between the three of us, we had about three hundred dollars. We ordered all kinds of stuff! Some of it we ordered just to see if we would like it. Marty would send stuff back 'cause he saw a guy in a movie do it once.

He had a plan to pass himself off as twenty-one so he could get into a real card game. He kept saying "twenty-one" over and over, 'till Mark slugged him and told him to shut up. We finally ate ourselves sick and it was time for some fun and games. Marty played "Space Invaders" all night. I walked around and watched some of the other kids play. Mark found a game of computer football and proceeded to exhaust his funds.

It just seems like every time you start having fun, it all ends way too soon. We left the club and looked up and down the street, Bars were rockin'. One had a great band jamming their heads off. Mark said he liked that kind of music

Then Marty started going on about "The Clash."

"These guys are really good but they're nothing' compared to The Clash." he bragged. Punk music was coming on the radio and it was right up Marty's alley. Loud and wild.

We couldn't get into the club, so we stood outside to listen. When the music stopped, Mark and Marty decided to go get the car while I waited to see if the band would start playing again. It all seemed like it got quiet all at the same time, so I walked around a little. There was a back alleyway, but it was too dark to see very far. I looked around and saw a bright red glow from a cigarette back in the shadows. All of a sudden I heard a voice say,

"Hey Hip Rich, what's up? Man, it's been awhile."

"Hello?" I said. Then out of the darkness came Lance Cawlings. "I don't believe it!" I said. He shook my hand as I looked at him. His face was road-weary, but his hands were strong and steady.

"I saw a friend of yours a while back. Let's see, where were we? Oh yeah, doin' a gig in Houston. She's a doll, man! Cutest chick in Houston, I'd wager. She said to give you a message." He dug through his wallet and came up with a piece of paper torn from a phone book.

"She told me if I ever ran across you to tell you..." He leaned into the light and read the note. "Oh yeah. She said, 'I'll be home soon. Save your kisses for me.'" He handed me the note and smiled. "Now I'm free from that riff and the rest is up to you, my man. Don't let love get away from ya." He looked at his watch and said, "I gotta get back. It's our last set."

Then he turned and walked back into the shadowy alleyway and disappeared. "Floored" isn't the word. I was electrified. I reserved raving at Mark and Marty, joyously keeping all the news I got waiting for them and running into Lance Cawlings. It was fun keeping it to myself. I suddenly thought of Kate Ridgeway. What now? Torn and confused, it stayed with me all the way home. I couldn't sleep, I couldn't concentrate.

Spring was waning. I was bored with everything in school except drafting. I didn't know what to do. Wendy really tried to get hold of me, but Kate and I were pretty close. I just tried not to think about it, but it hung on and was always in front of me. Marty and Dagmar were out of their minds waiting for school to end. The last week of school was nuts. I've never taken so many tests in my life. My right hand had a groove in it and a sore spot where my pencil sat as I filled in circle after circle on the dopey answer sheets. Finally, it was all over. I only had days until my sweet Wendy came back to her true love, ME! Or so I thought. Marty kept trying to convince me I was an alien spy.

"Then I'll wait for my ship to arrive so I can fly away to my home planet forever!" I laughed.

"That isn't funny, man! You know how deeply concerned I am about the alien counter-culture that wreaks havoc on this dying town."

Dagmar chimed in and said, "Let's build a go-cart."

"You know Martus, I was talking to Miss Ellie, our junior high yard dog, and she has something special in mind for you." I loved teasing him.

"You know Richie Boy, there is a limit to our relationship. Your willingness to joke about the aliens among us makes me feel ill at ease." I looked at him and started laughing my head off. "It isn't funny!" He said, stifling his own laughter.

We looked at Dagmar and she said, "No. Really. Why don't we?"

"Why don't we... what?" Marty asked.

"You guys never hear me! It's as if I'm one of the 'alien invaders!'"

Marty yelled at me, "See what you've started!"

Just then, Myrtle blew through the door with two pizzas and a load of root beer. "Let the feeding frenzy begin!" she yelled, then looked at us and said, "Charge!"

Marty called this "The desolation of Italy."

"Pizza doesn't come from Italy, Zit Skull" I chortled. "It's as American as apple strudel!"

"Do I have to teach you everything?" he said, choking down another slice. He would roll the slice of pizza up as tight as he could then shove the whole thing in his mouth. Dagmar called it "Amazing!" I just stood there dumbfounded at how much he could get into his mouth all at once.

"No really, why don't we make a go-cart?" Dagmar was not going to let this slide. I looked at Marty and then it happened. Just like it always does.

His eyes got real big, he looked off into some unknown place and said, "Yes. Oh yes! It can be done."

Dagmar smiled. "I love it when you brainstorm Marto." She smiled coyly as she spoke. With that, she and Marty started this gross pizza kiss.

"Come on. My appetite is running amok," I protested.

Myrtle walked in and said, "You two ought to join a kissing contest instead of this one." She held out an ad from an art magazine that Marty subscribed too. It was a full-page ad for the 10th "Annual Graphic Arts and Multimedia Contest." It was sponsored by art colleges, movie companies, and art stores all over the state. The prize was twenty-five thousand dollars and a three day seminar at an art college in Washington state.

"You ripped a page out of my magazine?" Marty said. Then he looked at his aunt and smiled. He set his root beer down, gave Myrtle a hug and kissed her on the cheek. A big pizza kiss. She didn't even protest. I would have, but that would have been with or without a mouth full of pizza.

"Thanks, Myrt." Dagmar was way ahead of Marty and was already filling in an entry form from inside the magazine.

Marty barked, "Come on, man, that's my periodical."

"There's more than one in the magazine, Mr. Periodical." I looked at her and realized I'd never even heard her mention a family or brothers or sisters or anything. "Dagmar, can we meet your folks?" The room went still. She stopped writing and looked at me.

"Please don't ask me about my parents. I know you didn't mean anything by it, but I just can't talk about that right now."

I felt a little embarrassed and weird, but then I just dropped it. She went back to filling in her form for the contest. Marty started in on his entry form while drawing a go-cart. Once the contest app's were all filled in and sent away, we plunged into the go-cart fantasy with both feet. Myrtle let us rip her lawnmower apart. I started gathering stuff to make a frame.

"All you have here is a bunch of old scraps." I said.

Marty's neighbor, Mr. Crow, saw us and came over to see what was going on and say "Hi" to Myrt. He told Marty to go into his side yard and see if there was anything he could use. Marty ran over and began rummaging around. About twenty minutes later, he emerged with a go-cart frame, wheels intact and ready for an engine.

"This guy has more crud back there than a junkyard," Marty laughed.

"I thought you might find that. It's been back there since last year." Mr. Crow said. His voice was kind and friendly. "Listen Marty, it looks like you're going to get this done in the next couple of days or so. I consider this mine. If you do anything dangerous, I will take it back, motor and all."

"Thank you, Jack" Myrtle said. He will be safe and I will be with him."

We looked at her and I asked, "You're going to be with us?"

"I want to ride it!" Myrt laughed.

I think I found the common link between Marty and me. We worked our guts out putting that go-cart together. By the time we finished, Dagmar was sketching the activity! Marty and I went inside and finished off the pizza. None of us ever touched that go-cart again. I think it's just the doing that Marty and I liked. Once it was done, we just moved on to something else. Marty got in some kind of bummed out mood for some reason when Myrtle told him he was going to clean up the mess before anything else.

Marty shot back "When pigs fly out my butt!"

Myrt walked over and pinched the soft meat on his arm.

"Ooww! Crap, Am I a melon that you need to see if it's ripe…?"

"Don't you use that language in my house!" Myrtle barked.

"That hurt!" Marty scowled.

"You don't ever give me any of your fat lip, Buster Dude o' Boy! This is my house and you live here. If I tell you to do something it better get done Mr… Snip." She was waving her finger all over the house while she spoke.

Dagmar chimed in and said. "Yeah, me too, 'Buster Dude o' Boy!'"

Marty rubbed his arm and looked sad. "Myrt could you make, like, a real nice dinner for us?" he moaned, rubbing his arm.

"Well, Honey, what would you like?" She quickly got all soft, and spoke in a motherly tone.

"How about some "Twisted Go-Cart Wreck Myrtle Souffle?"

Marty was still the big wise-n-flip when he wanted to be.

Myrtle grabbed a magazine and chased Marty all over smacking him with it. They seemed to be having the time of their lives. The phone rang and Marty yelled, "Saved by the bell!"

Myrtle held the phone after her greeting. Her face went blank. "Is she at home?" Myrtle asked. "Which hospital is she in?" Dagmar stopped painting. Marty went over and stood by Myrtle. "OK, well, thank you for letting me know." She hung up the phone and looked at Marty. "Your mom is in the hospital, Sweetheart." Marty's face was telling. He knew why without asking. He left the room by himself.

I asked Myrtle "What happened?"

"Marty's dad got ahold of her while he was all liquored up. He pulled a bunch of her hair out and beat her with a cane. She has lacerations all over her back and shoulders. She's just messed up."

There were no tears. Just a feeling of helplessness that came over the whole house. Oddly, Myrtle got into her car and went shopping. Dagmar went to find Marty and I fell asleep on Myrtle's couch. When I woke up, Dagmar was sitting across from me drawing a picture of me sleeping. Marty was in his room sketching an alien. The house was filled with the smell of baking lasagna, and for a while I just laid there and stared at the ceiling. I wondered why my mom wasn't calling.

Just then, Myrtle came in, looked at me and said, "Your mom called. I told her that you're still breathing and you're going to have dinner with us." I got up to go wash my face, then headed for the table.

"Man, I'm hungry" Marty said as he walked into the room.

"All you guys do is eat!" Dagmar said as she sat down and loaded her plate.

Myrtle always made us have a moment of silence before we ate. We got about halfway through dinner and I was losing my mind, so I finally blurted out,

"Shouldn't we be going to the hospital?"

"No!" Myrtle shouted. "Both if those people are drinking themselves to death. It's beyond my heart how they cannot know how much hurt and anguish they cause themselves and other people. One of these days, one of them is going to hurt or kill someone because of their stupid drunken crap!" She got up from the table and left the room.

"I'm so sorry," I said. That was the end of that. Myrtle was deeply hurt by Marty's folks and their bad behavior. It was just better to leave it alone.

The art contest was at the end of August. Marty and Dagmar both worked alone on their projects and would not let anyone see what they were doing. Not even each other. As the summer got on, we started migrating to Mark's house. We hung around the back patio and made up games to play. One of Marty's favorite games was a version of "Trivial Pursuit" he made up called, "If You Don't Know the Answer, You're a Slime Rat!"

It consisted of Marty acting like the host of a TV show. He would stand in front of everyone and ask questions about movie stars. Then we had to get up and imitate the star while we gave our answer. Dagmar left the room and Mark threw orange gummy bears at Marty. I sat there and read a book I found sitting on the kitchen table titled, "If You Don't You Do." One of Mark's mom's friends published it himself. It was a self-help book. In it he advised his readers to divest themselves of their old bad habits and take up kick boxing. Up 'till then, I enjoyed reading. Mark invented a game he called "I Can Tear Out Your SSinuses." We were supposed to sit across the room in a chair while Mark threw a football at our faces. No one wanted to be the first to be "It." It was all pretty dull until Mark's older brother James walked in.

"What now, Magic Marker, are you going to show your friends what a big football hero you are?" Mark jumped up and started swinging his fists at him, then one of them landed.

I never saw Mark get angry at anything. It was pretty weird. Both of them fist fighting and calling each other names. Suddenly Mark's mom and dad came running into the room and pulled them away from each other.

"I'm not taking his crap anymore!" Mark yelled

"Poor King Baby! Daddy's little favorite. What now football hero? Ya gonna speed off in your new car?!"

Mark's mom told them both to stop. What struck me is she said it in this calm cool voice and they both did what she said. Mark was made to read to his brother and help him with his night school. It seemed odd to me cause Mark didn't even start the whole thing. I knew not to try and talk to Mark about it. He just got all mad when Marty tried. It was a hot issue in the DeVerge home so I just stayed out of it. Besides, I had enough to think about. It seemed like Wendy should be home soon and I didn't know what to say to her or Kate.

By the second week of August, I was almost out of my mind. Heading into our senior year, Wendy and I missed all three years of high school that went before. Then I found out that she and her family were back in town and she would be in school! My beautiful Wendy was so close, I had to see her face. I sent Marty on a spy trip to her house. He was supposed to bring back any info about the doings over there. He sure did. He even saw and talked to Wendy! She said she didn't want to see me at all, that I never wrote her or answered the note she gave to Lance Cawlings. That she and Carl Simms were seeing each other and Her aunt told her and her mom all about what I did.

"Is there more? I swear Marty you better start talking. Or I'll tell your Aunt Myrtle about that night at the tree fort!"

I was the only one who knew that Marty was smoking on occasion. I caught him at the old tree fort we made one night, puffing away. Dagmar had told him if she ever found out he smoked she would never talk to him again. I had a barrel over his head but I never used it 'till now.

"Start talking, Shale!" I said as I stepped toward him.

"Her aunt told her mother that you already got a girlfriend and now you were trying to juggle Wendy and Kate so you can have two babes at the same time."

I sat down and began stewing. Just the thought of her lying to Wendy and her mom like that was more than I could bear.

"There's more, Richard." Marty said. "Her aunt accused you of roughing up her cousin Scooter. Wendy said they keep a close eye on her and they are going to put her in home school to keep her away from you."

I couldn't believe what I heard. I just got up and walked home. I walked slowly, deep in thought. I wanted to protect myself but now this was way beyond wanting to see Wendy. This might even have some long-term problems that hang over me for a lifetime! When I got home, I thought maybe I should try one more time to talk to my dad and I figured that maybe since he was not under as much pressure as before, he might listen better. Plus, I thought if I approached him in the right way, it might make a difference. I walked in the front door and straight into his office. "Dad, can I talk to you man to man?"

Mom came in and said, "Hello, Stranger. Your summer must be up and running. Haven't seen you in a while."

"Dad. Mom. There's a pretty serious problem I think you should know about."

"Go ahead, Richard," Dad said as he eased his way around the desk and sat down next to my Mom. I explained the situation and told them the things Wendy's aunt said about me.

"She told Wendy's mom that I was trying to have a girlfriend and now I'm trying to get Wendy under my hooks so I can have two. She also accused me of child abuse! I never did any of those things and I think I deserve a chance to clear my name in front of my accuser." "I learned about this in civics, Dad. I'm being falsely accused! Now I want my time in front of the person who's accusing me."

Mom looked at my dad and said, "Lee, this time I'm going to act. This slanderous stuff is ugly and unfair."

He looked at her and said, "I'm with you."

I went to my room and waited to hear what might become of the situation. I couldn't believe they responded the way they did! Up 'till now, they just acted like I was a little kid with a crush and at some point I'd get over it and move on. I waited for an hour. Then Marty called to say that he and Dagmar were contacted by the art counsel sponsoring the contest and it was time to take their art to the contest headquarters. He wanted me to go. He said that they would pick me up in the morning around 8am. I didn't really want to go, but I told him OK.

Eight AM came sooner than I wanted, but I got ready. Marty, Dagmar, and Myrtle pulled up at about eight thirty. We had a great day. Marty also included Mark so all of us took the art work to the judging center. We found tons of people there! They did everything in alphabetical order. All the artwork got set up and covered in white sheets with different colored lights shining on them. Then the final judging dates were announced. Myrtle took us to lunch. After lunch we all went to the mall.

"Well, I guess I can collect my twenty-five thousand dollars in about two weeks!" Marty bragged.

Dagmar looked at him, patted him on the cheek, and sighed. We stood on the edge of the top level and watched people shop. Myrtle was buying a blouse, so it took a while. As I looked down and let my eyes wander through the crowd, I caught sight of Wendy. I hadn't seen her for a long time. She looked beautiful. I felt a weird sort of sick feeling come over me, like I wanted to cough up a psychedelic yawn, but not really.

She was with her aunt and mother. Marty saw her at the same time.

"Don't go down there, Richard, it's not time," he warned.

"I have to," I said.

He put his arm around me and said, "I don't use this a lot but I'm going to now. I'm an artist. I know when to stop and step back, when to add color and when to let it be what it is. Richard I'm telling you as a friend and brother, don't go down there. It isn't time."

Just then, Myrtle came up holding open bags full of stuff. "Look! I got all of this on sale." She looked down at the theater and her eyes got real big. "Let's go to a movie." My stomach turned to mush. I looked at Marty. He looked at me.

Dagmar came up with a pretzel and said, "Look what I got!" Mark and Marty gave each other some kind of sign and Mark started acting sick.

"I think I'm gonna faint in a minute!" he moaned.

"What does that mean?" Myrtle asked.

"It means he's about to swoon." Marty answered.

She knew what that meant. So we hustled Mark out of the mall and my two friends, who were as close as brothers, saved me from a fate worse than death. The next two weeks went by pretty fast although Marty would NOT stop bragging about his artistic range.

"No one can beat me! I won this contest hands down!"

We just let him "crow" as Myrtle put it.

She seemed to know something, but wasn't letting on.

Finally the day came. All of us jumped into Myrtle's car and drove to town for the final judging and public unveiling. The place was alive with artists and movie people. Graphic artists and computer animators were there. There were schools, booths and scouts from all over. We spent some of the day talking to animators from Pixar. Marty got some autographs from people I never heard of. Then the time came.

We packed into a big auditorium. These people were as hardcore as it gets. There wasn't a second or third prize. You either won or you lost, all or nothing. It was wild and exciting. The first thing was the unveiling. All the covers were removed from the art that was going to be judged. Then the public got to walk around and look at the art. Marty's work was first on my list.

I went straight over and worked my way through the crowd. My mouth hung open as I approached and looked at Marty's drawing. It was stunning. Marty had drawn a sketch in pencil with some charcoal and light pastels of Leonardo D' Vinci painting the Mona Lisa. It was sort of a side view so you could see his face and her face at the same time. I didn't even know what to say. It was so alive you could swear it was moving. Everyone that walked by said the same thing. It was "Blindingly beautiful," as one woman put it.

I went to see Dagmar's artwork, but I could hardly get through the crowds. People were waiting in line to see her work. I finally got up to her painting and I nearly fainted. Dagmar had painted, and drawn, a multimedia picture of a city. What was so incredible is the city was a light gray sketch. Some very light pastels tinted it perfectly. The city stood on the edge of a lake. The reflection was all in color. It was out of this world! Her hand was so light it just reached out and touched you. Every line complemented the whole. Every stroke made the picture dance. You could see the water moving. You could hear the city breathe. It was more than I can put into words. As the big moment arrived, we all shuffled into our places and waited for almost half an hour. My legs were killing me, but I stood and waited. Mark kept nudging Marty.

"You got it, Bro.'" He kept saying.

A man came out, made a speech about the arts, and then introduced Martha Landis, the Director of this year's contest.

"Well, the moment you've all been waiting for has arrived. All the artwork here today is beautiful, and I'd like to thank all of you for entering your wonderful work to this, the10th annual Graphic Arts and Multimedia Contest. Judging this year was very challenging, and all of the entrants were contenders. Our winner this year is the painting titled…" She opened the envelope and read the name: "'City by the Sea,' by Dagmar Taylor!"

"It's Dagmar's painting! Dagmar won!"

Marty said over and over. Dagmar was red-faced with the whole thing. She walked up to the podium and was given a check for twenty-five thousand dollars. She thanked everyone she could think of, then walked backstage with Mrs. Landis and some of the stage hands. Marty was silent. All of us were numb with excitement. After about fifteen minutes, Dagmar came back out with some papers and the check. She smiled at Marty. He stepped over and hugged her. He said,

"You're just too beautiful, inside and out."

She started crying and they went off by themselves for a little bit.

The ride home was full of football stories and a new art contest. Marty's braggadocio was in full swing. In his rather vain attempt to imitate Terry Malloy, he kept saying, "I coulda been a contender."

As we pulled into the driveway, we saw the lights were on.

Myrtle said, "We didn't turn any lights on.

Marty, did you leave the lights on?"

She thought for a second, then pulled the car out of the driveway and went to Mark's house. He lived closest to Marty. Once we were stopped, she asked to use the phone, we went inside, and called the police. We stayed at Mark's house until we heard back from the cops. It seemed that someone had gotten into the house and torn up Marty's art.

"It can't be Dad. He's still in jail for beating up my mom."

Mark stayed home. The rest of us met the police at Myrtle's house. It was a mess. Marty's art was in shreds. We got asked tons of questions, then they left us to clean up the house. I felt sick for Marty. He seemed to take it all in stride. Dagmar helped Myrtle clean and Marty went into his room to check the damage. For whatever reason, Marty's room wasn't touched.

"Maybe whoever did this was in a hurry." He said.

Then he looked at me and smiled. "What a night! My girlfriend beat my pants off in a contest I was sure I'd win. Then I come home to this." Marty looked around. Then he looked at me. "Richard I think I need to be alone."

Chapter 7

TRUTH AND LIES

Mark DeVerge was "The Man." The school year that introduced us to being seniors in high school brought him in touch with scouts from every major college in the country. I went to the games so I could watch him play and hang out with him, Marty, Dagmar, and Kate after the game. One Saturday evening in late September, our school was playing against the best high school in the state. They hadn't lost a game in two years. They were divisional champs. Our coach and theirs were old buddies. So for the fun of it, they had the two teams meet for a game.

It was a big night and the air was full of wild excitement. Mark was told by his folks and the coach if he didn't help his brother and keep the peace he would not play. I suppose he did what he was supposed to do 'cause he was suited up and on the field. However, I could also tell that things weren't good between Mark and his brother James. He was not at the game and Mark's other two brothers Jason and Craig were. I could not begin to tell you what happened on that field. Mark was just "on." He told me once that sometimes you get into this "zone" and you can feel the entire field. You just know what to do.

This must have been one of those nights. Mark could not do anything wrong. He blasted that ball from his hand like a bullet all night! He never once threw a bad pass. He didn't need a lot of time. He would just fade back and let that ball fly. It was absolute magic. The other thing that was great for Mark that night was some of the college scouts got wind of this game and came to watch for future talent. I think they got what they wanted.

At one point, the opposing defense had our team pinned at their thirty yard line in their territory. It was third down and fifteen. Mark broke the huddle and the guys lined up. He counted off beat and threw the other team off, which made them jump. They got penalized five yards and our team got a first down. Mark huddled the guys up again. This time he did a quick count. The ball was snapped. Mark faded back and blasted that football almost in a straight line to "Lion" Williams. Smack right in the middle of his chest, a couple of steps into the end zone and boom! Touchdown! There were flags on the field though. One of our team got called for holding and they had to do the play all over again.

Mark didn't flinch. He broke the huddle and started his count for the snap. Both lines jumped and the defense called a blitz. They all came at him from everywhere. Mark had nowhere to throw the football. All of a sudden, he just *ran!* He tucked the ball under his arm and ran. The crowd was up, screaming as the foot race for the goal line saw Mark dodging, jumping and running as fast as a horse. I watched in awe as he broke tackles, twisted and ran. It was wild.

The closer he got to the goal line, the louder the crowd became. It was now a foot race with Mark out front and a defensive secondary player named Ray Dunn. Ray was catching up to him and the screaming crowd got louder and louder. Ray caught Mark, but it was too late. He was feet from the end zone! He pulled away from Ray, jumped, and broke the zone right at the goal line where he was finally brought down.

Touchdown! This time it was good. Mark never blinked. He just played a game he loved and understood. It was great!

That night we all went to the DeVerge home and had a very late supper. Mark talked about the game but never talked about himself. Except for the tension between Mark and James, that's how the whole family was. Just wonderful people, kind of good humored and fun. As the night got on and the food ran out, Mark looked at me and Kate, Marty, and Dagmar. He said, "I got you all something." He walked across the room, opened a cabinet, looked at me, and said, "You first." He handed me a box, all wrapped up.

"I wrapped it myself," he said, smiling his big Mark smile.

I unwrapped it and looked into the box. It was a third edition copy of *The Pickwick Papers* by Charles Dickens. "Look inside," he urged. I opened the book and there, quite faintly, was the signature of the Author's son, Charles Culliford Boz Dickens. I was floored.

Mark said "It was my grandma's and she left it to my mom after she died. I told my mom I wanted to get you something that was really special and she gave me that book. We all know how much you love to read."

"Mark, I don't know what to say." I looked at his mom and said, "Are you sure you want to part with this?"

"All it does is sit on a bookshelf I know my mother would want it to be somewhere special." Mark's mom was so sweet I just gave in and said "I don't know what to say."

"Well I do, Man. Thank you for being such a good friend, Richard. I hope we can be friends forever." Mark smiled. Then he did the same for Kate, Dagmar and Marty. He handed them each a box and said, "Come on! Don't keep me waiting."

Kate got a bracelet that she saw once at the mall. Mark remembered how much she liked it so he got it for her. I watched her open it and felt guilty for the secret I was carrying around. I just couldn't let my feelings for Wendy go.

Mark and Dagmar both got the same thing. It was a beautiful artist's toolkit with new supplies like pastels, pencils, erasers and a whole list of stuff.

"Now, when we do this in our family, we have to get up and say what we are thankful for. You first, Marty." Mark spoke with authority. "No wise guy stuff," Mark said as Marty got that look on his face.

"Umm. Well, I'm grateful most of all for my Aunt Myrtle who has saved me from a very sad life. I thank her every day in every way I can." When Marty was done he sat down as fast as he could.

"You're up, Dagmar!" Mark said. She stood up and turned red-faced. "I don't know what to say," she said. "Wait, yes I do." She looked around and spoke. "My mother put me up for adoption when I was born. I was raised in foster homes 'til I was sixteen. When I couldn't stand it anymore, I ran away and changed my name. I was in an intersection begging when Myrtle found me. I hadn't eaten in three days. She took me home and introduced me to a woman who helped me and supports me with a small place to live and art classes. I not only found a family in all of you, but I found a great guy to love. I hope this is real." She sat down and wiped the tears from her eyes. I knew it was my turn. I stood up with Kate and it got real quiet.

"Well, we really feel good about having such good friends, and..." Just then I was interrupted.

"No Man, get real!" Mark said.

"Ok. Ummm well, I love all my friends,and I feel really weird and goofy right now. . all of you are just great." I felt so weird. I started to swoon. I sat down and got all red-faced.

"OK Mark. You started this. Now it's your turn!" Marty said.

"Wow Rich it's almost like your birthday. Tell us about your birthday Richard." Marty knew how much I hated my birthday. "Come on Bro". "Richard doesn't like his birthday and he won't let his mom celebrate it. He doesn't ever like being the center of attention. "

Katie looked at me and said, "Come on, let's hear it."

Marty laughed. "Oh no! It's clown time!"

"It's Mom's fault she had to hire "Wee Wee the Clown," I laughed.

"Richard, Marty said it wasn't 'Wee Wee.' It was 'Oui Oui Le Bouffon.' He was a French clown." "He was drunk as it gets, that's for sure. He said he was on medication. I could smell the med's on his breath! 'JD Old Number Seven.' He passed right out on Richard's cake. Oh brother! what a mess!"

"Rich, why don't you like your birthday?" Dagmar was not going to let me off the hook.

"I don't like being the center of attention. I don't want to be."

"OK, that's right. I love you guys. I was pretty rough on you in junior high and I hope you'll forgive me. I love my Mom and Dad. I really love the life they gave me. And one more thing." He paused and looked down, then raised his head and said, "Damn! I was good tonight."

We all threw our napkins at him and laughed. After that, we played livingroom football. This is where you wad up about five socks to serve as a football. Then we picked teams. Kate, me, and Dagmar were on one team. Mark and Marty were on the other. The trick to this game is, you have to play on your knees.

The ball is snapped and what occurs next is sort of a sock riot. All of us scrambling around on our knees, knocking the crud out of each other to try and get a wad of socks. It's bizarre what girls do when confronted with the overpowering strength of a male competitor. Kate and Dagmar nearly beat Marty blue. Then they tried to jump Mark so he couldn't throw the ball. Kate explained, "You guys are stronger than we are, so we have to use more tricks!" Dagmar agreed. So the brutality continued until I threw up. "Vomiting puts a damper on everything," Marty concluded.

I felt stupid for throwing up, but Marty and Mark kept poking me in the stomach the whole time we were playing! I could only stand so much, no matter how fun it was, I just hurled. I never vomited and laughed at the same time before.

Mrs. DeVerge came in and made us take a break. I helped her clean up the half-digested remains of my dinner and apologized a thousand times. She looked at me and said, "I always regret letting Mark do this, someone throws up every time!" I thought she was joking.

I looked at Mark and he smiled his big ol' Mark smile. "You did this on purpose?" I said.

"It's not for the faint of heart, my friend." Then he threw the wadded up sock at Marty and both of us jumped Marty and yelled, "Dogpile!" We got up, grabbed our gifts, and said our "Good-nights."

The football team won the championship. The season ended. January came up fast and I was getting sick of waiting. So I started yelling quotes from my new book.

"You are very amiable, no doubt, but you would be charming if you would only depart." ..."Love is the most selfish of all the passions." ..."The merit of all things lies in their difficulty."

"My God, Richard, what are you reading now?" Mom said.

The Three Musketeers" I said. "It's a love story, if you read it right."

"Well, if you'll join me in the living room this evening, I have some information that might get this all straightened out."

"You know something? Come on, Mom, please? Can you give me a hint?"

"Richard, just be here at five and we will discuss this with you." She was serious, and I knew it. I roamed the house, I took a nap, I showered, I read, I even tried pacing. I hated that. Finally, it was 5 pm I walked into the living room where my mom was sitting with a cup of coffee. I sat down and said, "Okay, what's up?"

"I was able to speak to Wendy's mom tonight. She's having a terrible time with Wendy, and her sister isn't helping."

"That sister of hers is a liar and…."

"Just hold on, Mister. She told me that Wendy was diagnosed with bipolar disorder." "Richard, did you know that Linda James was sexually harassed at her job in Colorado? Did you know she went to Texas to retrain so she could keep a job even though what happened was not her fault? You've been feeling pretty sorry for yourself for some time. I thought you might need a different perspective."

"Look Mom, if this is some kind of guilt trip then maybe we better end it right here. I was lied about and my name was dragged through the mud and no one has yet come to my defense."

"I told Linda what happened and she said she'd try to do what she could. That was all I could do."

"That's it? If someone did those things to you or your company - there would be lawyers everywhere! But when it's dopey Richard? Oh well, he's just a kid. He'll get over it."

"I gotta land with Richard on this one," Samantha said as she walked past and out the door.

"Richard, that woman lost her husband. She's raising two kids by herself and she was taken advantage of in the worst way, almost losing her job. Now she has to deal with a daughter who is emotionally sick. Do you want me to drop another bomb in her life?"

"No, I want to tell Wendy and her mom that I did not do all those things. And I want to see Wendy."

My mom handed me an envelope and said, "Wendy wrote this for you. I hope it helps." She got up and left the room. I opened the envelope. The note inside was not good news. Once again, I was being shafted by Wendy's aunt and there didn't seem to be anything anyone could do. It read:

You know Richard, I wrote you so many letters and you never answered any of them. Aunt Rachel says there are just some men that treat women badly. I really thought we had something we could hold onto, maybe even forever, but I guess Kate Ridgeway took my place. I guess we should just forget it! Maybe someday we can be friends.

I sat there and stared into space. I just had to let it go for now. Maybe life will take a turn for the better or maybe God will feel sorry for me and strike me with lightning. But for now, I was without hope. The Beatles asked, "Do you believe in love at first sight?" The answer is, "Yes, I'm certain that it happens all the time." That's how I felt. That's what I knew about Wendy and me. We loved each other right off, but I couldn't fight lies and separation.

I was hardly in the mood for Marty and Dagmar they started dancing around Marty's room to The Sex Pistols. They both jumped around like two rabid dogs. So I called Mark and he came and got me. I was stunned when he pulled up. He was in a 1977 Pontiac Trans Am Classic.

"Oh man, where did this come from? That's real sweet, Mark."

"Yep! My dad got it yesterday. I asked if I could take it for a spin. Hop in."

"Oh man, Dude! The force is with you! Is it used?"

"No way, Bro! This ride is brand new. My dad says if I even get a bird turd on it he'll have my head."

"Hey! Let's go over to Little Eddie's Big One. I'll buy you a burger. Are you hungry?"

"I'm always hungry. Let's go!"

On the way there, I told him what was going on with Wendy and her mom. As we ate he sat and looked at me, not really responding. Then he got all weird and said, "I got into it with my brother James last night. He's getting worse, I think. He can't really read very well and he's frustrated. My parents make me help him, but he gets all mad and starts throwing his books around."

"What books?" I asked.

"He has to go to this night school for people who can't read. He has books he has to read and write reports on. They're pretty simple. Anyway, last night he was trying to get through one of them. I was sitting with him for what my mom calls "moral support". My dad walked in, looked at me and said, 'Evening Champ.' Before Dad could say anything to James, he went berserk. He threw his books and started yelling at everyone. He pointed his finger at me and said, 'I hope you die!' That's when I started yelling back. He came at me and we had to get pulled apart by my two other brothers. It was pretty bad."

"Did you hit him, Mark?"

"Yes. It was all so crazy, I just don't remember. He always calls me names and makes crappy remarks. I know things are hard for him, but it isn't my fault."

We finished our lunch and Mark drove me the long way home. I felt a little better as I watched him drive away.

Chapter 8

WHERE ARE WE?

I was never into all the social groups at school. The Band Geeks, the Cowboys, the lunch room Klingons, and the So'shes. I had a hard time with the Jockstraps, but I loved hanging around with Mark and they didn't seem all that bad. So I had to let go of some of that. Really though, the kids that were the most obnoxious, in my book, were the Dopes. That's what Mark and Marty called the kids who smoked pot.

Marty already knew what drugs and alcohol did to people from firsthand knowledge of his own family. Mark, being in sports, wouldn't get near anything like that. He said his dad would hang him high if he ever found out he took drugs. I was always just antisocial enough not to want to get involved with too many people at once. So the three of us made a great team.

After Dagmar won the big contest, some guy that called himself an "artist manager" moved in on her. She fell for his line and moved away with him! Marty was pretty depressed, so Mark and I made a day to go hang out with him. Our senior year was just about over and school for us was kind of slow. So one Friday we jumped ship, forgot about school, and I drove us to Marty's house.

When we got there, Myrtle was chasing Marty around, whacking him on the head with a magazine. It was a riot watching her try to hit him. He was a good foot taller than her and she had to jump to get to the top of his head. It seems Marty just couldn't keep himself from blurting out whatever smart remark popped into his head. I had recently told Marty to read more.

"You'll get more ideas for your art if you read," I told him.

So he buys a giant box of old comic books at a garage sale and starts reading "Superman" and "Green Lantern." One was called, "The Adventures of Jack the Ripper." Old "Mad" magazines and a small pile of something called "Alien Mother-in-Law." Well, these ended up all over the floor. Before we got there, Myrtle went into Marty's room and looked around.

"What is this all over your room?! Look, you're eating in here. I have told you not to eat in your room. Oh my God, Marty! This comic has whipped cream all over it. What is this?"

"It's dessert," Marty told her. She grabbed a "Mad" magazine and started beating him with it. That's when Mark and I showed up. These scenes only lasted for a few minutes, then Marty would beg her to make something great for dinner. It was a psychotic relationship, but both of them got something out of it. You could tell they loved each other.

We were not permitted to go into Marty's room until he picked it up. So me and Mark hung out in their built-in patio until Marty emerged and announced that his room was fit for human habitation. Marty promised that the comics were not all over the bed anymore so the three of us piled into his room. I took a look around. The room was pretty nice looking. Then Mark looked under the bed. It was stuffed underneath with comics.

"You promised, Man. Look at this mess," Mark said.

"I told her they weren't on the bed. I didn't say anything about under it," Marty told him.

I flopped on the bed and found a comic wrinkled under a pillow. "What's this?" I asked.

"I didn't know that was there," Marty replied with a smile.

Mark started raking comics from under the bed and stacking them in order. Marty busied himself with his sketch pad.

"So what's up with Dagmar?" I said, still leafing through a gruesome copy of "Alien Mother-in-Law."

"Hey look!" Mark laughed, "A copy of 'Ladies Home Journal' magazine." He sat down at the end of the bed and started flipping the pages. "Oh man! You guys should see this!" Mark laughed. "It's a test for women to give the men in their lives. It's called, 'Does He Really Love You, or Does He Have a Roving Eye?'"

Marty sat, seriously occupied, as he sketched a picture of Mark looking through the magazine. "Ok, you guys. I'm going to ask you these questions. Try to answer them truthfully." Mark instructed. "Question number one: 'Do you look forward to being with me?' "Question two," Mark said, "Do you like my hair its natural color? Or should I dye it a mysterious color like brown or red?'"

"What's so mysterious about brown?" Marty asked. "Everything is brown."

"Question three," Mark continued, "'Do you like the clothes I wear or would you prefer me in clothes that other women wear?'"

"At the same time." Marty quipped.

"Check out this question!" Mark said, as he fell back laughing, "Do you like small breasts or large ones?"

Marty grabbed the magazine from Mark and threw it across the room. Just then, Myrtle came in. When she opened the door, the smell of her burgundy chili filled the room. All three of us jumped and made for the kitchen. We hit the bedroom door at the same time. Mark used his arms to power through the door first. Myrtle's burgundy chili is worth dying for, and she made a double recipe, complete with sweet corn cake. None of us could move by the time the feeding frenzy was over. So we sat and talked. Mark asked where Kate was, and why she hadn't called yet.

"She had to catch up on her homework," I told him. "Her mom said, 'No anything until she's done.'"

Then I yelled, "I know! Dagmar was kidnapped by an alien werewolf!"

The room was quiet for a while. Then Mark said, "You should spend more time reading women's magazines. Then you'd know more about them. You should have paid more attention to the test I gave you."

"What test?" Marty said.

"You know! The one I was reading. Now she thinks you're Peter Pan." Mark smiled and jabbed Marty's arm. I put my head down and started laughing.

"Well, if I'm Peter Pan, you're Tinker Bell!" Marty shot back.

Mark looked at Marty, then we all just laughed. I always thought it was really odd how Marty handled adversity. I guess he just had to, from an early age. Once in a while, he'd talk about his folks. It was never very good. He seemed to know how to separate himself from the feelings that could have ruined his life.

It's weird how things go when you're thinking about someone and they walk into the room or call. In this case, Marty's mom, Lottie, showed up at Myrtle's front door. We heard voices and Marty's face went blank. She walked into the room and didn't even recognize Marty. Her eyes were bloodshot and she could hardly walk in a straight line. She looked at all of us and yelled, "Where's my boy?" Her speech was slurred and she kept leaning on the wall. I felt sick for Marty and just sat there, not knowing what to do or say.

Then I saw something that taught me a lesson. Mark stood up, walked over to Marty's mother and took her arm. He gently led her to a chair and helped her sit down, all the while saying things like, "It's alright. I'll help you, just lean on me." Myrtle had tears on her face and was hardly able to speak. I looked at Marty and wondered why he wasn't in a rage. He looked at me, then at his mom. Myrtle got some coffee and gave it to her sister.

"What has he done this time?" Myrtle asked.

Marty's mom started crying. I mean really crying. It was all I could do to stand there. She kept crying, and then, through the desperate sound of her sadness she said, "Donna's dead." Lottie's face was a mask of grief.

Marty's face dropped and then, in firm resolve he said, "How did this happen?"

"She took some sleeping pills and drank some vodka." Her voice sounded sad and strained.

Myrtle looked up at us and said, "You boys need to go somewhere for a while so I can deal with this."

Mark was still by Lottie's side. He patted her on the shoulder and said, "I'm so sorry for your loss." There wasn't much we could do, so we made our way outside and stood in Myrtle's driveway.

"Marty, I don't mean to sound stupid, but Donna was your sister, right?" I guess I was so busy dealing with myself or school or whatever. I just never remembered hearing her name.

Marty looked at me and Mark, He shrugged and said, "They forced me to erase them from my life. It's like they're all someone else's family. I swear to God, if it weren't for Myrtle, I'd be long gone. If it weren't for you guys and your families…" He paused, then said, "They just lost everything. I feel really sorry for them, but I just have to separate myself."

Mark's dad pulled up in his Trans AM and yelled to Mark, "Hey! There are scouts at the house! Hop in!"

Mark said, "I hope things work out," slapped Marty on the back, and was gone.

Me and Marty started walking. No destination seemed planned, but we ended up at my house. We went into the living room and sat down. Marty thought he might dye his hair and change his name to "Farlen Coal" so no one would know him during our senior graduation.

"That won't work! You'll still have the same face!" I said.

"I'm planning several nose jobs before school ends," he said, looking in the mirror as he fiddled with his nose.

"You're in home school, 'ya dunce!" I hollered.

"I'm not in home school, you slacker!" he said. "Myrtle got me into an art school where I can finish my senior year and study art. But I can still be in our graduation."

My dad yelled that he was trying to work and maybe we'd better find something constructive to do. Marty said, "Yeah, we can go get your car!"

"What's my car doing at Marty's house, Richard?"

We walked back to Marty's and I drove home. Whatever Marty was up to, or going to do, our senior year was almost over and the end of our school career was upon us. Marty's art was amazing. Mark's life of football was written in stone and I didn't have a clue what my future would be…

Kate got all caught up on her homework. All of us got buried in tests, Marty met a girl he liked, and Mark was getting ready to visit colleges. The end of our senior year was pushing us different ways and directions. Marty was in one art contest after another, Mark went to a college football camp, and I spent as much time reading and with Kate as possible. I don't know what we did, but it was all so fun.

It went by in a flash. Kate started talking about the senior prom. I got to thinking what might happen if I didn't end up doing anything? I loved drafting, but I was also good at wondering why people are all crazy. I thought about being a psychologist, but I couldn't stand listening to anyone complain.

My sister Samantha got a certificate as a veterinary assistant and left for Colorado. Lyn was one year behind me in school and devoted to joining the Red Cross.

Mom and Dad were a little better off money-wise and I made a little cash helping Kate's mom with her paperwork and chores around the house. It was so rare to hang out with each other! The only time we really got together was at Mark's house for our first Sunday of the month dinner. This time, Mark had a girlfriend named Shannon that he was friends with at school. I guess they decided to see each other a little more. Marty came with Allison, his new love, and all of us had a blast.

Mark's dad made prime rib. He cooked it for, like, two days! We had a moment of silence, and then the munch fest was on! Everyone took turns telling what they wanted to do over the summer. We all stopped and looked at each other. Suddenly, our last days of school were upon us.

Chapter 9

YOU CAN'T GET IT BACK

Myrtle got Marty into an art trade school during our senior year. His contest earnings had been mostly socked away, and she put up the rest. Mark DeVerge was over at my house a lot. Mark found out that he needed a shop class to graduate on time, so he chose drafting. He wasn't good at it and he didn't like it at all. Fact is, I did most of his work for him. Marty wanted me to help him and Allison paint a mural on Myrtle's garage door.

"Really, Marto, if you were me, what would you do? Hang out with a cute girl or smear paint on somebody's garage door?" Marty called Kate and told her his plan. She thought it sounded great, but asked what would happen if we didn't get it right. Marty just shrugged and said, "So I'll fix it!"

So I got my mind changed for me. As long as I got to be with my friends, I felt that the occupation was worthwhile. It came to our attention, however, that Myrtle was out of town. She had no idea Marty was re-painting her garage door. I wondered out loud and often if we weren't all headed for putting her garage door back the way it was. Marty gave each of us a small part of the door and told us what to do.

So we spent our spring break, or a good portion of it, painting Myrtle's garage door. It seemed like a long time. Myrtle finally got home. She had been helping her sister relocate as far away as possible from Marty's father. After the death of their daughter, he was perpetually too drunk to see about funeral arrangements or even go to the funeral. Marty's mom just left. After years of abuse, she finally stopped drinking and was trying to put her life in some kind of order.

Myrtle was helping all she could, but as she said, her first priority was Marty. We had just about finished the garage door when her ride pulled up. I could hear her as she was getting out of the car.

"Oh my goodness, I *love* it!" She went on and on. "Oh my goodness! This is simply beautiful. Marty, you're so full of color and light! I'll never repaint this!" She made the neighbors come and look. I wasn't sure all of them were as thrilled as she was. "Oh, my land!" She hollered, then ran over and kissed Marty and then each one of us in turn.

"I guess she likes my work," Marty said, smiling.

Kate thought the whole thing was wild and wonderful. That night, Myrtle made a big dinner with an Irish cream pie for dessert. That was just about the only time Marty and I did anything together for the whole senior year.

We all went to Spring Dance though. Mark led the team to a 21 to 14 victory. Then Kate and I went to her house. We sat in the dining room on a small sofa.

"What are you thinking about, Richie?"

"How nice it is to be alone with you. I wish I knew what to do." I said.

She smiled and said, "You mean, you don't?" I got pretty mixed up and turned all red. She laughed and said, "Is that what you meant?"

"Umm…Well no, I mean like, for a future or whatever."

She looked at me and said, "What do you want to do? Richie, I want to tell you something." She spoke in a soft voice. I looked into her eyes and she smiled. She looked at me. I mean, right into my eyes, and said, "I have a confession."

"What?" I said.

"I think I'm falling for you."

I sat up and looked at her. I felt sad, but something had to be done and now seemed like the time to do it. "Kate, I think I need to go."

"Aren't you feeling good?" she asked me. "You had a long day painting so maybe you need to rest."

"Yeah, that's probably it," I said, standing up and heading toward the door. It all felt pretty awkward, but she got me home and said, "Good night" with a kiss on the cheek.

The rest of the year went sailing by. It's great to be a senior, but it'll be great to get out of school altogether. Kate planned "her" prom as she called it, right down to the last detail. She, Alison, and Shannon went to stores and made notes and talked over and over about what gowns they were going to wear. Shannon was so excited to be part of the whole scene. Her early life was marred by sadness. Her mom had breast cancer. She survived, but it put a real strain on the whole family. Things were better now. Her mom's in remission and she has what she calls "Real friends."

Allison's family was all good. She had four brothers and sisters, and they all thought Marty was some kind of genius. I couldn't get over that. Of all the people in the world I thought should go nuts and end up in some kind of weird crime spree, Marty was at the top of the list. It all seemed too good to be true. It wasn't all that late when I came home, and Mark left a note for me to call him. "Hey, what's up?" I said as he answered the phone.

"I got a full scholarship to Northwestern!" he said. I could hear the excitement in his voice. "Richard, you helped me make my dreams come true. You got me through those awful drafting classes!"

"Oh man, Mark, that's something. That's great!" I couldn't hold back. "Mom! Dad!" I yelled, "Mark got a full scholarship to Northwestern! We should party or celebrate!" I told him.

"After prom," he said, "All of us should get together, go somewhere special, and just enjoy life." I agreed.

Our plans were sketchy, but all set. The prom was up. We wanted a limo, but Mark wanted to drive in the car his dad bought him, and he wanted to escort all of us himself. We agreed. Kate took care of what she and I were going to wear, what kind of corsage she needed, and when I should be at her house. I arrived right on time. Kate's mom answered the door.

"Hello, Mrs. Ridgeway." It felt so formal. It *was formal*! So I thought everything I did had to be formal. I even called her "Ma'am" when she invited me in. I sat for a moment until I heard Kate's voice. "Are you ready?" I stood up and Kate came into the room. I was completely stunned.

"Damn, Kate, you look like a princess!" I suddenly realized what I'd said, and could feel myself blush. "Uhh... Sorry." I whispered.

Kate's mom said, "We'll let that one slide. She does clean up real nice."

Mark came to the door and off we went. It was all magic. Kate didn't talk to any other guys the whole night. We danced every slow dance, and when the prom was over, we went to an incredible restaurant, "Chez Chateau." They serve great food! I had shrimp cocktail for the first time. Amazing stuff! After we ordered, I looked up and in walked Wendy with Carl Simms. I was dumbstruck, they even walked over to our table to say hello.

There were no two ways about it Wendy and I locked eyes and didn't even notice anyone else. We couldn't avoid each other so I said, "Hi Wendy."

She looked at me and her eyes got misty and she spoke in a tone you couldn't miss. "Hello Rich. It's so good to see you."

"It's good to see you too, Wendy."

Carl Simms broke in and said, "Take a picture, Buddy, it lasts longer."

Wendy stepped back away from him and asked him to stop being rude. Marty spoke up and said, "Man, Simms, are those your armpits I'm smelling or is the food here stale?"

Carl took Wendy by the arm and walked away. It was obvious to one and all the chemistry between Wendy and me...was still there. Kate noticed, and the rest of the evening she was distant and cool. Mark tried to restore the good cheer and we all played along. Marty and Allison were picked up by Myrtle, so it was just Mark, Shannon, Kate, and me. We dropped off Kate and I walked her to her door.

"It's pretty clear how you and Wendy feel about each other Richard. Please don't call me again. I think you need to get your head and your life together." Then she closed the door behind her.

She wasn't wrong. I just turned and walked away. My house was next. Mark pulled up and said, "Hey, thanks for everything! Tonight was great. I'll always remember this. I hope you get things worked out."

I slapped him on the shoulder, said "Good night" to Shannon, and walked on into the house. It was one thirty am. When l got to my room, I was so tired I could hardly get the rented tux in order. I fell into bed and soon was fast asleep.

It doesn't matter how old you are. Everyone knows when the phone rings at four thirty in the morning, something is wrong. I just knew it was trouble. I could hear Mom answer the phone. I heard her say, "Oh my sweet God! That can't be!"

I heard my dad say something, then their voices got real quiet. I got up, slipped into my jeans, and went into the den where my mom was just hanging up the phone. Her face was wet with tears. "What's up?" I asked.

Dad looked at me, then at my mom. A tear rolled down his face. He put his head down, then looked up at me again. He said, "It's bad news, Son."

"Does someone want to tell me what's going on?" I asked. Now the queasy reality of what began to crystalize was hitting home.

"Richard!" he began, "It's really bad. Mark and Shannon stopped at a red light last night after they dropped you off. When it turned green they started to go through the intersection and a drunk driver ran the light going the other way. He T-boned the car, Mark was killed instantly, and Shannon is in critical condition. They don't think she'll ever walk again."

"That's not right! I was just with them! They brought me home, Dad. I'll show you! Here, let me call and talk to Mark. He might still be sleeping, but I'll show you Dad! I'll show you!"

I simply could not accept this cruel new reality, I was speaking with such resolve, I grabbed the phone and started dialing Mark's number. My dad reached over and stopped my hand. "Richard, Honey, Mark is dead." He spoke very softly and held my hand down.

"He just got a scholarship! He's going to Northwestern! He's with Shannon, Mom! He had everything ready! I helped him with drafting… it's not fair! It's not fair…Dad." I stood there with my fists clenched, yelling and crying. I desperately wanted to stop time. Go back and replay the night so Mark would still be alive. Still be with us. Still be my friend."

My dad is a man that just looks at life as, "You get what comes and you deal with it the best you can." He isn't given to emotionalism. I looked at him. He had tears in his eyes. "Richard, Son, I am so deeply sorry."

My mom had her hands over her face, crying. The room was dim, awash in a pall of deep sadness. There was nothing more to say. I went to my room and put on my clothes. It was still early, but I had to go to Mark's house. I remembered the way Mark helped Marty's mom and how kind he was to her. I walked out, and for the first time in my life, my folks didn't ask where I was going.

I drove to Mark's house and knocked on the door. Mark's brother, James, answered. His eyes were swollen and red. "Richard, I didn't mean it, I just got mad. I didn't mean I wish my brother was dead. I didn't mean it that way!" he kept saying.

Mark's mom came to the door and put her arms around him. "Come on, Jimmy Honey."

"Mom, I didn't mean it!" She motioned to me and I went in. Mark's dad was there. He was completely stunned and looked lost. My mouth opened, but I couldn't speak. Mark's mom came in after sitting James down and hugged me.

She looked at her husband. "He hasn't said a word since…" Her thought trailed off.

"Mrs… I… well…" I couldn't say anything. My words choked on tears I couldn't stop.

I gave her a hug and left. I didn't know what else to do. I made my way to Marty's house. It was still very early. The neighborhood was quiet, but my thoughts were way too loud. I knocked. Myrtle answered the door, a look of "I told you so" rage creased her face. Marty was at the dining room table staring straight ahead. His eyes were red and swollen.

"I guess you heard." I said, as I sat next to him. He wouldn't speak. He just looked into the distance. I sat with him. "How could this be?" I whispered.

Marty looked at me and said, "My dad killed my friend."

"What?" *Your dad*? What's he got to do with it?"

"He was drunk, as usual, on his way home from the liquor store. He ran a red light and killed my friend!" His face twisted in pain and fury.

"Your dad was the one that hit Mark?" I couldn't believe what I was hearing.

"I thought he was in jail!"

Myrtle spoke up and said, "I've been warning him for years that he was going to hurt or kill someone. Now he's hurt and killed in a way that's too painful to think about." She burst into tears as she spoke. She left the room, crying.

I just sat there with Marty. We sat silent for over an hour. Then he got up and called Mark's folks and explained to them the details of what had happened.

There was nothing more for me to do. I just felt a little lost. I said my goodbyes and went home. Lyn came and hugged me when I walked in. Mom was in the kitchen and dad was in his office on the phone. I sat down by myself and looked out at the morning. "I don't know what just happened," I thought. I had seen Wendy, lost any chance to have any kind of closeness with Kate, and lost a dear friend to a stupid drunk. Is this what it's like to be an adult? I had just graduated and all of a sudden my life was filled with tragedy.

Chapter 10

THE LONG STREETS HOME

I thought about Mark and his father, the riff between him and his brother. I thought about his mom. What's it like to lose your baby to a senseless act? She'll never see him again. Tears rolled down my face. I don't know what I want. I don't know where to go. My mom walked in sand looked at me. "I don't have anything to say to you that will help you Richard. I love you so much. Maybe you need to reach out to the person you want to talk to the most."

She ran her hand over my head and then walked away. I sat there empty and sad. It took some time but her words sunk in. Wendy! I have to go find Wendy. I would go talk to her and her mom. I got up and once again walked out the door. This time I was on my way to a place that was long overdue for a confrontation with the woman who had been lying about me. It was way past time to tell Wendy what really happened. I knew I had to face her mother. She had her own pain in that she lost her husband and was raising two kids by herself. Some creep at her work got way too fresh with her and she was dealing with a daughter who was not entirely healthy. I got to Wendy's house and

Carl Simms was still there. "Holy crud! Does this guy ever go home?" I thought. I knocked on the door and waited. Carl opened the door.

"Look Allen, Wendy is *my* lady and you need to get that into your head right now!"

The door was pulled open further and Wendy's mom looked at me. She smiled. I got up my nerve and said, "Mrs. James, my friend is dead. I'm tired and angry. I've been lied about and treated like I don't matter long enough. Please, Ma'am, please let me talk to Wendy so I can clear my name."

Carl Simms' face was all twisted up in anger and he looked confused. Wendy's mom looked inside and then said, "Please come in." I was stunned.

Carl looked at her and said, "Mrs. James, this is the monster that yanked around your nephew and tried to kill me!"

"Carl," she said, "I think you better leave now. You've been here all night."

For whatever reason, I was able to keep my mouth shut and let things simply happen. Carl stepped out and I stepped in. I almost laughed when Wendy's mom shut the door in Carl's face. "That boy just turned into the thing that wouldn't leave!" She seemed to be speaking to herself, so I didn't agree or anything. She brought me into the kitchen and we sat at the table.

"Mrs. James," I said, "I don't know how this works or why. But I love Wendy. I guess I always have, like, since I was born. I said something I shouldn't have said to your sister and it started this whole thing. I was getting letters from Wendy just after you went to Colorado, but after a while they stopped. It turns out that your sister found out from Carl that he was supposed to be bringing those letters to me 'cause Wendy wasn't supposed to write me or anything. Instead, she paid him two dollars a letter to give them to her. Carl told me that she kept them in a big cookie jar in the kitchen. I would have written Wendy every day if I could have. I even ran away to try and find her. I never yanked Scooter around by his arm. I was leading him out of the mall 'cause he almost burned it down and I thought we better get out there before someone caught on and we all got in big trouble."

I stopped and looked at her. She stared at me and then she laughed. "You poor thing. Sounds like the world got you by the tail and turned you every way but loose!"

I was kind of floored, but it made good sense to agree, so I did. She got up from the table, walked over to a cabinet above the refrigerator and opened it. Inside there was this huge cookie jar with a painting of fruit on it which confused me, but this was no time for analysis. She stood on a little stepladder and pulled it down. She pulled it close to her, came over to the table, and sat right by me.

She smiled and said, "The moment of truth." She opened the lid and looked inside. Her eyes came up to mine. She reached in and pulled out a big bundle of letters bound with three rubber bands. She held them up and said, "I believe these belong to you, Richard." Then she handed me Wendy's letters, all of them. I just looked at them and said nothing. "Young man," she said, "I think there's more injustice that's been done to you, me, and Wendy, than meets the eye. I'm wondering if you will let me talk to Wendy and I'll see what I can do on this end. I can't promise you what Wendy will do, but I think we can get most of this straightened out if you'll let me."

I wasn't sure why she needed my permission, but this whole thing with me being quiet and letting things happen was working pretty well, so I said, "Yes Ma'am." As I stood up I said, "Mrs. James, I have a lot of reading to catch up on. I think I'll go home now and read these letters. They're addressed to me." She walked me to the door and I was soon on my way.

I pulled up in front of the house and thought I should call Mark and tell him what just took place. Suddenly a wave of grief hit me, tearing through me with unrelenting hammers of reality. Mark isn't there, he'll never be there again. I can't call my friend. I felts anger and rage. It came out of my face. I hit the dashboard. I yelled, then my door opened and my sister Samantha was kneeling down beside me hugging me. "It's Ok, little brother, I'll take you in. Come on."

She helped me out of the car and into the house. It was odd. Sam always just treated me like her dopey little Brother. Something inside of her must have understood I was stunned and grief-stricken. I couldn't call my friend. He was dead.

When she got me inside, my mom heard us and came in. Sam just sort of left the scene. Mom just looked at me, wiped a tear from her eyes, and stood there. I sat on the couch and suddenly heard my grandpa's voice inside my head. "Life isn't fair, Richard. Sometimes it's downright crappy."

My mom hugged me and said, "There's nothing to say Sweet Boy I wish so much there was."

I felt an arm around my shoulder. My dad said, "I'm not unfeeling, Richard. I just want you to have some perspective. Think about how Mark's family feels. As sad as you are, his parents just lost a child." He walked away, saying "Those people must be devastated."

I stood there trying to gather myself. I'm sure I heard the phone ring, but the things that went on outside of me just seemed distant. I heard Mom say, "Why don't you come to dinner over here tonight? Okay Linda, that sounds great." She hung up the phone and made sure I knew to be there later this evening. "Linda is coming over with Wendy."

Suddenly I started analyzing and worrying I started wondering what we should have for dinner. Aren't girls weird about eating stuff? Like maybe they don't want to eat spaghetti in front of anyone 'cause the spaghetti noodles could get stuck in their cleavage? Like, if it fell off the fork or something? One time I was eating spaghetti at Marty's house and he got it all up his nose. He was sitting there talking with noodles hanging out of his nose. I've always suspected he did that on purpose, but he denies it.

Once we had to have dinner with one of my dad's clients. So we're all at this guy's house. I mean me, Samantha, Lyn, Mom, all of us. They served spaghetti. This guy is loading spaghetti onto his fork by the gross. We're all sitting there, he gets a snout full and all of a sudden his face went red. His head goes back about four feet and he sneezes his lungs out! I mean, spaghetti went all the way to the lunar surface! Samantha swears she still pulls spaghetti out of her hair every now and then to this day. Lyn got the worst of it. She had meat sauce all over her face. Then a big gooey blob of spaghetti dripped down into her dress. Sam and I still call Lyn "Spaghetti Face" when she gets out of line. His wife nearly died of embarrassment. Would have been worse if it had been Dad, I suppose.

We ended up leaving kind of early. When we got home, as I was getting ready for bed, I reached into my pocket to get any loose change or stuff I wanted to keep. When I pulled my hand out, it had spaghetti all over it. I'm not kidding! There was a trail of spaghetti from his house to ours, about eight miles of it! My dad says he found it on the floorboard of the car and my mom swears she found some in her purse. So I was just thinking that maybe spaghetti wouldn't go so well. I was freaked out. I had spent so much time trying to get to Wendy! Now that she was coming to me, I didn't know what to do. What should I say? I was so preoccupied I *walked* over to Marty's. I forgot that I could drive. When I got there, Marty was in his room, drawing. I walked in and stood there, staring at him. He pretended not to notice me.

"Look, Man, I have alien friends all over this town and you are on the shortlist for abduction." I began.

"It isn't funny!" He shot back. "Every twenty minutes I get this empty, twisting feeling in my guts. It's sick. Mark was our friend. How can he not *be* here anymore?"

"I don't know, Marty. I thought the same thing. I just want your help and maybe that will take our minds off the sadness for a minute or two."

"Okay, Richie-Rich. What's on your mind?" He set his pencil down and looked at me. I stood there and stared at him. "Well are you going to speak or stand there posing for an idiot statue?"

"You're a little off your game, aren't you?" I replied.

"Under the circumstances, you might give me a break. Now que pasa? Give me the grit, will you?"

"Wendy's going to be at my house this evening. Marty, I don't know what to say to her. I don't know what to do."

He smiled and said, "Look, just act like you're living with a rabid wolverine and her cubs. You'll be so freaked out nothing will bother you!"

"Do you know how stupid that is?" I said.

"Do you want my help or not?" I sat on the edge of his bed and looked at him.

"You know what Richard? We only found out about Mark a few hours ago. Maybe that reality can give you some perspective. It looks to me like life just throws stuff at you and you either deal with it or you don't. I can't tell you what to say to Wendy. I didn't know what to say to Mark's parents when I went over there this morning. But they seemed to be okay with what I *did* say."

"You went to Mark's house this morning? I thought you called."

"The line was busy," He said. "I told them it was my dad who hit Mark. I told them how deeply sorry I am and I wish I could do something. His dad didn't hardly move and his brother James is messed up bad."

"He seemed messed up when I went over there, too."

"James kept telling Mark he wished he was dead." Marty just looked at me. This half smile came to him, then he said, "You know, you've been in the Wendy chasing business for so long that you never gave it any thought what you might do if you ever caught her. All of us have suffered a big loss. Go home and sleep, Richard. Things will seem clearer when you wake up."

I did what he said. I went home and fell into bed.

Chapter 11

FINDING WENDY

I Woke up to the sound of voices. I looked at the clock. "Oh no! It's after five!" I said out loud. I jumped into the shower and got out as fast as I could. I made sure I looked and smelled my best. I walked out into the living room. A woman from down the street was there with her daughter selling Girl Scout cookies. The look on my face must have spoken volumes.

"Well, I see you were expecting someone else!" the woman said. Mom bought some cookies and they left.

"I asked you to wake me up a little before five, Mom."

"Richard, Honey, take a look at the clock"

I looked at the clock in the living room. It was only three thirty. I slumped back to my room and started reading. I decided to read from the end of the book to the beginning. "It is a far, far, better thing that I do than I have ever done; it is a far, far, better rest that I go to than I have ever known." I grew weary of this right away.

So I tried reciting literary quotes from movies. "Let them die and decrease the surplus population," I called out. "To the last I will grapple with thee! From Hell's heart I stab at thee, and for hate's sake I spit my last breath at thee."

I even started acting out the parts as best I could. "Why was I not made of stone like thee?" I leaned against my bedpost feeling the cool stone of Notre Dame touching my skin. "'But, soft! What light through yonder window breaks? It is the East, and Juliet is the sun. Arise, fair sun, and kill the envious moon!'"

"Wow Richard! You really are a dope." Samantha and Lyn were sitting on my bed, watching me.

"Thank you for the unsolicited critique. Now get out of my room!"

"Richard there's nothing else to do!" Lyn complained.

"Mom!" I yelled. "These two shlogbots are in my room proving what illiterate slugs they are."

"You know Richard, they're the only two sisters you have. You should try to..." Before I could complain about the fact that she was always defending them, the doorbell rang.

"What's that?" I called out.

"Oh, that's funny! He can quote Shakespeare, but he doesn't know what a doorbell is." Sam laughed as she walked out.

Wendy's mom called and asked if they could come at four instead of five. Wendy is getting used to some new medication and it makes her tired. I hurried to the door and opened it, expecting to see Wendy for the first time since she moved. There was Mrs. James. I looked out around her and then stood silent.

"Wendy is not going to be here Richard. She just isn't doing real well. May I come in?" I let her in and asked her if she was thungry.

"I don't know what you mean!" She laughed.

"I mean thirsty or hungry."

"No, I'm fine thank you."

I didn't understand the awkwardness. Earlier we got along real easy. Now it was like swimming through crude oil. Dad came in and sat next to me. He introduced himself, then Mom finally came in and said. "Hi Linda! I'm so glad you could come over. Are you thungry?" Mom looked at me when she said "thungry" and smiled. "I guess Richard is a little nervous. I'm sorry about Wendy. Was she doing any better before you left?"

"A little. I'm proud of the way she's dealing with all this. There's so much I would change if I could."

They seemed to be on a whole different wavelength. I wanted to reconnect with a beautiful girl I cared about and they were off on some other planet talking about something I didn't understand. I almost got up and left. I didn't know what to do so I raised my hand. They stopped talking and looked at me.

"Richard, do you want to say something? You don't have to raise your hand" Mom seemed a little surprised and Mrs. James smiled.

"I want to ask if Wendy is well enough to have a visitor. Namely, me?"

"Well, Richard, at first they thought she was bipolar, but I recently got her to a new doctor and she said that Wendy is suffering from anxiety disorder."

I forgot all about dinner. When the doorbell rang I was feeling like Wendy finally made it. I ran to open it and found a kid I knew from school standing there with a couple of pizzas.

"Oh yeah umm, well, come on in and drop those right here. I motioned to the kitchen counter and he walked over, put them down, and stood there. I stood there and he stood there and looked at me, then put his hand out. I shook his hand and said, "Thanks for the pizza." He stood there and smiled. All of a sudden, I realized he wanted a tip. I reached into my pocket and found a quarter. "Here ya go!" I said. "That should do ya." He looked into his hand, then looked at me. Just then Dad walked in, handed him three dollars and said, "Alright, fast delivery, very nice." He turned and left and with that the food fest was on.

Wendy's mom told us about leaving Colorado and driving to Texas. It sounded crazy. She had a cool way of telling stories, so it was great to listen to. I was aching to see Wendy when I realized I had left her letters in the car and didn't read one of them. I jumped up with a mouth full of pizza and ran out the door. Wendy's letters were right on the front seat where I left them. I grabbed them up and ran back into the house. The folks were now all kicking back in the living room and hardly noticed me as I blew past.

I threw myself onto my bed and opened the letters I was deprived of for so long. I read them all. Some twice. My heart ached to think how Wendy felt when I didn't answer her. Every syllable, every phrase, all the pleas and the questions as to why I wasn't responding. It made me so angry and at the same time so insane to get to her! I must have been reading for a long time. I could still hear Wendy's mom and my folks talking and laughing. Then, in a flash, the lights all went out. "Oh no!" I heard my dad say, "The electricity has gone out!"

I needed no time to think, no time to make any choice. I jumped up, reached under my bed, grabbed my emergency candle and ran. I blazed through the house past the folks and out the door. I didn't want to take the time to mess around with the car, so I ran. I ran like little Jimmy Gramaldi from "Invasion of the Body Snatchers." My favorite sci-fy. I ran like the crazy man Aticus Finch told Miss Maudy and his kids. Tom Robinson had run like I ran, through the darkness of a town without light. A town stripped of its identity, without the recognition of landmarks lying in darkness, waiting for what was meant to be. I was a man with a cause that had eaten his soul long enough. I finally found myself at Wendy's front door. I knocked softly and waited. I heard a voice say, "Who is it?"

I said, "It's the man who's going to light up your heart forever!"

"Go away Carl! I don't want to see you anymore."

"It isn't Carl, Wendy. If you still want to be a dancer, I'll dance with you for the rest of your life." I couldn't believe what was coming out of my mouth. The door cracked open slowly and there stood the treasure I fought so long and hard for.

"Wendy... I didn't get your letters because your aunt paid Carl to give them to her. But I just now read every one of them. I have a lifetime to answer them if you'll let me."

She opened the door all the way. "Oh my God, it's really you!" she whispered. "But I can't let you in, my mom isn't here."

"So come outside with me. It's kind of dark, but I have a candle and June looks beautiful framed around your face."

She smiled and stepped outside. "Rich I'm so sorry about my aunt. I nearly lost you 'cause of her. I thought about you and us so much, then this morning I heard about Mark and Shannon. She was a friend of mine. I just got mixed up and I didn't know if I should..."

"Shhhhh! It's okay." We looked into each other's eyes for so long. Then, ever so softly, our lips touched. For the first time in my life, I felt as if I was right where I always belonged. The moment reigned softly. As our eyes opened, all the lights came back on. It was as if the night heard my broken heart and caused the lights to go out just long enough. Long enough to finally find what both of us were looking for.

As the kiss ended we were hit by glaring headlights. "Well I guess I got here in time." I heard Wendy's mom say. I thought for sure we were going to get shellacked. Mrs. James said "Come inside both of you and let's get a few things straight."

We sat at the kitchen table and Wendy's mom sat between us. "All right, you two! If you promise to follow a few rules, I'll be on your side always. Rule number one: No kissing when you're alone. Rule number two: Remember that I'm here and I want to be part of your lives. And please take Danny with you once in a while. He needs some male influence. He grew up without a father and he needs to do stuff that gets him away from his mother. If you can do that, it would mean a lot to me."

The agreement was in and Wendy thought we might have time to go see Shannon's parents at the hospital. Her mom drove us to my house so we could get the car. Wendy wanted to know how this happened. I told her how I found out, and about Marty's dad. She was angry, too angry to cry. We arrived at the hospital just in time. Wendy found Shannon's mom sitting near the ER.

"How's Shannon?" she asked, taking her mom by the hand.

"She's a little better," her mother said, "But we won't know just what we're dealing with for a few days. She is expected to survive though." Her voice was steady but subdued. We told them what we knew about Marty's dad. Shannon's dad came over but never said anything. Soon after, we left.

We went to Mark's house next. As soon as Wendy saw Mark's mom, she broke down. Mrs. DeVerge hugged her for a long time. Mark's dad was still in the same place, just sitting there silently, in solitary grief.

Days crawled by. Wendy and I barely left each other's side. I dreaded Mark's funeral. Hoping this was all some bad dream, I kept thinking I might wake up and find everything the way it should be. That was not going to happen. Mark was dead and Shannon was in the hospital, with a long recovery ahead.

It was time to say "Farewell" to Mark. The whole football team was there. The scouts from Northwestern came. Marty and Myrtle were sitting with the DeVerge family. The rest of us sat behind them. I almost got up and left more than once. I didn't want to acknowledge that Mark was gone, for real. I felt bad about being glad when it ended, but I was still relieved to go.

Out in the parking lot, Mark's parents called us over. Me, Marty, Wendy, and Allison stood there, around Mark's folks. His mom invited us to come for dinner on the first Sunday of every month, just like always. Mark loved that, so we decided to keep that date as a memorial for our friend. We all agreed and went back to Marty's house. Myrtle grabbed the mail on the way in. There was a letter from Marty's mom. Marty's dad was arrested after the accident and had a big legal mess in front of him. It was suggested that he might end up doing five years.

"Five years? Is that all!?" Marty yelled.

"It's a plea bargain, Marty," was all Myrtle would say.

"Mark is dead. Shannon is crippled, and he might end up only doing five lousy years?" Wendy said.

I didn't have anything to say. I've never understood people and the way they do things, including legal things. The afternoon crept by. We remembered Mark. Allison talked about Mark's mom and how she helped with suggestions for the prom. Marty kept saying we should do "something," over and over. No one could really come up with anything real. As evening came on, Wendy and I made our way home. All those mundane things seemed heavy and without very good reason. When we came in, my mom was in the living room. Wiping tears from her eyes, she was in the same state as the rest of us. No one could believe Mark was dead.

"Marty called. He wants you to call him as soon as you get home." From the way she was crying, I thought something else must have gone wrong.

I called Marty from the office phone where my dad was. He answered right away and said, "I have it! I know what to do!"

"What is it? I thought we went through as much as we could," I said.

"I'm going to paint a mural on the big gym wall at the high school in honor of Mark," he told me. He had a way of expressing his ideas as though they were a *fait accompli*. I thought about it but didn't say much. I was so sad and tired. I kept letting the idea float around my mind until Marty said, "Hello?"

"Yeah Marto, I'm here," was all I could come up with.

"It's a great idea! I'll get people to give donations and help paint! Myrtle and Allison will conduct bake sales as the mural goes along until it's done."

"Wow. Marty! Can this work?" I asked. It was a beautiful idea, a lasting memorial for Mark.

"Yes, but I need your help." He told me his reputation with most of the teachers and principals in the whole district was not really up to par. "I need you to help me so they will take me seriously." I thought about it, and told him we'd be over soon.

When Wendy and I arrived, we had my mom with us. Myrtle was so excited she was cooking all kinds of stuff. The house smelled great, and then about four pizzas arrived. "This is GSB central!" Allison announced. Wendy asked what that stood for and Allison put her fist in the air and said, "Give Something Back!"

"What does that mean?" I said.

Marty looked at me. For the first time he seemed like a grown man. "It means my father's sad excuse of a life caused me, my mom and sister, and Mark DeVerge pain and suffering. Soaking his head in a bottle was more important to him than his family or the people around him. He and my mom took away more from my sister and me than anyone can know, and he kept it up until he killed someone. In this case, it was a friend I loved and wanted to share life with. So I'm going to do the only thing I can think of to make some of that mean something. I'm going to paint a beautiful mural in honor of Mark's life and legacy."

We cleared a space on Myrtle's patio, and made room for Marty to draw plans. My mom called some of her real estate friends and got them on board. Myrtle made food. It wasn't long before her house was packed with people from all over town. I called one of the football coaches, Mr. Sack. No one believed his name was "Sack," but it was. I knew him from the football camp the summer I was the waterboy. He used to help me up every time one of the football players bowled me over. I filled him in on the plan and he was overwhelmed. He wanted in, and was going to come over right away. I was dazed at how fast this all took shape.

"It's getting late and it's been a very long day." Myrtle shouted.

Marty started mocking her "Ooooh it's so late!" He looked at his watch and said, "It's only eight thirty. The party is young!" She was already wailing on him with a magazine so the rest of us just carried on.

We called the superintendent, Mr. Trapp, but it was summertime and he was hard to find. Coach Sack called in a favor from one of the PTA folks and got Mrs. Cranes, his secretary, to get the superintendent's home number. She was not sure he could get the approval. None of the faculty she knew were all too pleased with Marty Shale and his antics over the years. They set up a meeting for Friday afternoon and would at least hear his ideas. I felt grim about presenting this on a Friday. I had always found Fridays to be odd and ready to strike. Marty said I was getting obtuse and he didn't want to hear about my weird Fridays.

"I already have a whole bunch of pictures of your ugly can at eighth grade graduation and that's enough for any man." He blurted this out right in front of everyone in Myrtle's house. Some of them didn't know about my exposure and wanted to hear all the details. Marty was only too happy to regale them with the gruesome event. After a long rendering of my most embarrassing moment, they all just stood there looking at me. Then Mr. Sack came across with his own albatross of shame.

"When I was fourteen, my parents made the trip from Flagstaff to Sacramento to see my mom's brother. It was a vacation trip for them, so they wanted to spend time with family. We got there and settled in with everyone, mostly girl cousins. I got up one morning to take a look at the gunner birds my sister told me about. She told me they only came out in the early morning, and you had to stand out by the storage shed in the buff and make a call. She taught me the call and I got 'Real good at it,' she said. So there I was, out by the storage shed first thing in the morning, naked to the world making this call so I could see the gunner birds. Just then, all my female cousins came around the shed. There stood my sister, right with them, with a smile she didn't let go of for about three months. You know, my daddy wouldn't do a thing. He said I got what I deserved for being so gullible."

I looked at my mom after he was done with his story, and she just laughed. After Mr. Sack saved me from being the only one in the room who was caught bare and red-faced, the crowd thinned. Everyone had assignments. We will meet again next Thursday. I left with my mom. When we got home, I got a call from Marty.

"Did you forget something?" he asked.

I thought and said, "I'm not sure." Then it hit me. "Wendy! Where's Wendy? Oh no."

"Her mom came and got her," Marty told me. "I don't think you're going to have a real easy time getting her attention again."

"Oh just when we were getting together I have to do something stupid and blow it all."

"Yeah, that sounds about right." Marty scoffed.

"What can I do now?" I knew I should apologize, but exactly how? I had no idea.

Chapter 12

IS LIFE GETTING IN THE WAY?

Thursday came around quickly. The whole group met at "GSB Central" and filled us in on how their assignments were coming along. All systems were "go" for Friday. I couldn't believe how it was happening! I was afraid something was going to go wrong. I anticipated the school board, who would decide if Marty could paint a really big mural on the gym wall, might vote "NO!" I tried not to think about it.

Myrtle made chicken enchiladas. We all sat and talked and ate while Marty brainstormed out his presentation for the board. We all helped with an idea that Allison and Myrtle came up with, to bring in some of his award-winning art. It was a long day. Marty is nuts, so everything takes longer. The day ended. It was time to go home.

Friday morning at nine all of us met at the Arts and Performance Center next to the high school. Marty's idea lit the whole town up, and everyone wanted to see what the end result would be. Once we all got settled, the meeting was called to order. The superintendent got up, made a short speech, and proceeded to explain Marty's idea. Then he asked if anyone wanted to express themselves concerning the mural. Mrs. Todd, Marty's eighth grade science teacher, stood up and walked to the front of the stage area near the members of the board.

"This young man has done nothing but disrupt classrooms, make smart remarks, and insult teachers for as long as he was anywhere near a school!" She continued. "I hardly think that a person of his ilk would be appropriate for this kind of project. I further don't see how a mural is going to make any significant contribution to this campus or this town with respect to the awful events that have happened here lately. The fact that it was a Shale that caused this tragic event should give all of us a clue as to the breeding of the entire family." She went back to her seat, proud and determined, and sat down.

After that, The Super introduced Marty so he could do his presentation. Marty walked up and unveiled a poster sized representation of what the mural would look like. Marty was pale and looked confused. He started to talk. Not much would come out. It got real weird in the room while Marty cleared his throat and kept starting over trying to explain his idea. It was then I saw Marty for what he was. This kid is an artist. He could do wonders with paints, sketching, or any creative work where he's alone with an empty sketch pad or paints. But a speaker? He isn't. He's not even okay. He just stood there, looking dumb as a rock. I got up and stood by him. He looked at me with pleading eyes and shrugged.

I spoke up. It wasn't too bad, 'cause I had a civics class where we had to address the class like in congress, and try to convince them to pass a law that we believed in. It was pretty much the same. So I stepped up and said, "Members of the Board and guests..." Everyone in the room burst out laughing. I was already into it, so I just went with the flow. "I've known Marty Shale for most of my life. His family was torn apart by alcohol abuse. His sister ran away, and Marty was blessed to end up with his Aunt Myrtle. There were a lot of things I didn't know about him at first. But as we got older, I learned how much he cares about his friends and how much he loves Myrtle. All of us are capable of change, and growth. Two weeks ago, a tragedy came into our lives. Mark DeVerge was killed by a drunken driver. Mark was loved and admired by his teammates, and was treasured by his friends and family. As it turned out, the man driving the car that killed Mark and injured Shannon, was Marty's father." The room got quiet and all eyes were fixed on Marty.

"Mark meant the world to Marty. They were friends and brothers." I continued. "It's hard to imagine how Marty felt when he learned that the man responsible for killing and injuring his friends - was his own father. So he made a plan to give something back. What could he give to his lost friend and the people left behind to mourn?"

By now, I was really into hearing myself talk. I was starting to get a real feel for public speaking, yet I knew this was for Mark and not for me. Just then, the chairman said, "Mr. Allen, can you get to the point?"

"Marty, and all of us, want to paint a mural on the big wall in the gym," I said, rather taken aback by his abrupt manner.

"What kind of mural would it be?" he asked.

"It would be in honor of our friend, Mark DeVerge, I believe it would have a sports theme. As you can see from the poster, Marty made us an example of the finished work."

It got kind of silent for a minute, then the chairman said, "We've seen your fantastic drawings out in the lobby, Mr. Shale, but is there anyone outside of your friends and family that can vouch for you?"

I thought my chin was going to hit the floor when a voice from the middle of the crowd answered, "I will!" Everyone turned toward the sound of the voice. Up stood Mr. Reichfeld, our junior high principal.

I leaned into Marty and said, "Isn't that 'The Third Reich?'"

He continued speaking. "All of you know the work I did at the middle school. Some of you have worked right alongside me. I've spoken with this young man and followed his progress ever since I met him. I was there when he won most of his art contests and I'm in the process of helping his aunt in her request for scholarships at two graphic arts colleges. Not only can he paint this mural, but I think he should. I know he'll do a great job that will make the DeVerge family and this town proud."

Mr. Reichfeld sat down and the room was still. The chairman spoke up and said, "Is there anyone else who has a dissenting opinion?" No one said a word. "Then with that, I think we can take a vote. All in favor, raise your hands." All the judges raised their hands. "It looks unanimous to me. Permission is granted for Marty Shale to paint a mural on the wall of the gym, in honor of Mark DeVerge." The room exploded in applause. The mural was on!

The results were out of this world. Marty outdid himself. He had lots of help. People paid as much as two hundred dollars for the chance to paint part of the picture! "Myrtle's Baked Goods" sold out and were gone every day before noon. The town donated really great goodies for Myrtle. All she and her friends had to do was sell them!

When it was all said and done, Marty's mural raised over six thousand dollars! The money went to buy paint and supplies. The rest was donated to MADD (Mothers Against Drunk Drivers). The mural started on a Friday and took four weeks to finish. It ended on a Friday. Not bad for a kid who had every reason to back out of life. I look back now and I can't believe how things worked out.

The time hurried by. Marty and Allison got married and moved to L.A. Why L.A.? Because Marty's talent got him a great job at Universal Studios in the graphic arts department. He bought a house and had Myrtle move in with them. He told her, "It's my turn to take care of you, Myrt."

I always laugh when I see his name on various movie credits. I love Marty. We still see each other on the first Sunday of every month at the DeVerge home. Yep, we still have dinner there. Mark's dad has never been the same. They keep a place at the table with Mark's picture there, and we talk about old and new times.

My dad had some trouble with his kidneys and they had to yank one of them. He's alright, though. My mom is the same. She likes it when one of the kids calls. My sister, Samantha became a full on veterinarian!. She moved to Colorado and works with horses. She checks in about twice a year. My little sister Lyn and I are close. I talk to her almost every week. She got her RN degree and a friend got her in with Doctors Without Borders. She always calls from exotic places.

Wait a minute, You're probably wondering what happened after I forgot Wendy at Marty's house the night of the GSB meeting. It took about three months! She was pretty mad, but her mom talked to her and told her she was being unreasonable. I got a job drafting custom homes for a construction company. I sent lots of flowers and candy. So one day I went over to her house. Her mom let me in and I took the tough guy approach. I walked right up to her bedroom door and knocked. I heard her say, "Come in."

I walked in and saw her sitting on her bed filing her nails in the middle of a whole room of flowers. "What is this?" I asked.

"It's all the flowers you sent me. I was going to wait another week or so and see how many flowers I could get."

"How many other strange secrets are you keeping from me?"

"I used to wait for you and Marty to get to the top of the quad near the lunch area and then when I knew you could see me, I'd walk across real slow." She looked at me and smiled as she spoke.

"Ok wait... what? You did that on purpose?"

"Well, I wanted you to notice me," she said.

"I still see you walking across the campus. It's something I'll always remember."

She blew off her fingernails and stood up.

"I'm sorry, Wendy." I stood there looking dumb.

She walked over to me and said "What for?"

"For hurting you. I just don't know how this ever worked, but I've loved you from the moment I saw you. I love you still."

"I love you too Sweet Boy, and God willing I will love you forever." She leaned forward and kissed me, my arms folded around her like they were meant to be. She pulled back and said, "But if you ever forget me again I'll shatter your world."

"I'll never leave you anywhere again." I meant it. She knew it.

Wendy's mom retired and is still living in the same house. We visit when we can. Wendy's brother joined the Navy, so we don't hear from him too much. Her cousin Scooter went into a diabetic coma and ended up in a wheelchair. Her Aunt Rachel died from some kind of virus. Her funeral is another story.

Me? Oh yeah. Well, I married Wendy and last month she delivered an eight pound three ounce baby girl with ten fingers and ten toes. I fell in love with Wendy when I laid eyes on her. That was a long time ago. At our wedding, Marty gave us the sketch he made of Wendy walking across the schoolyard at lunchtime. He made a frame and signed his full name to it.

The day Wendy had the baby, my folks were both at the hospital along with Wendy's mom. My dad was there when the nurse handed me our daughter. I was so scared I'd hurt her! She felt so fragile. I looked at my dad and he smiled at me. Then, for the first time in my life, I understood my father. I knew why he was the way he was. I stood in shoes that I never knew how to wear until I looked at that little girl. We named her Kathy, my mom's middle name. I wished Marty could have been there so I could finally answer his question: "What's your dad like?"

Well, that's pretty much it... "Goodnight, John Boy."

www.ingramcontent.com/pod-product-compliance
Lightning Source LLC
Chambersburg PA
CBHW030211130726
47898CB00012B/976